Angel
Angel

Angel Angel

APRIL STEVENS

Viking

VIKING
Published by the Penguin Group
Penguin Books USA Inc., 375 Hudson Street,
New York, New York 10014, U.S.A.
Penguin Books Ltd, 27 Wrights Lane,
London W8 5TZ, England
Penguin Books Australia Ltd, Ringwood,
Victoria, Australia
Penguin Books Canada Ltd, 10 Alcorn Avenue,
Toronto, Ontario, Canada M4V 3B2
Penguin Books (N.Z.) Ltd, 182–190 Wairau Road,
Auckland, New Zealand

Penguin Books Ltd, Registered Offices:
Harmondsworth, Middlesex, England

First published in 1995 by Viking Penguin,
a division of Penguin Books USA Inc.

10 9 8 7 6 5 4 3 2

PUBLISHER'S NOTE
This is a work of fiction. Names, characters, places, and incidents
either are the product of the author's imagination or are used
fictitiously, and any resemblance to actual persons, living or dead,
events, or locales is entirely coincidental.

LIBRARY OF CONGRESS CATALOGING IN PUBLICATION DATA

Stevens, April
    Angel angel/April Stevens.
        p.   cm.
    ISBN 0–670–85839–0
    1. Mothers and sons—United States—Fiction.   I. Title.
PS3569.T4397A83   1995
813'.54—dc20   94–20137

This book is printed on acid-free paper.

Printed in the United States of America
Set in Bodoni Book
Designed by Brian Mulligan

To Sandy,
my angel.

Acknowledgments

I am always grateful to my mother, Carla Stevens Bigelow, and to my father, Leonard Stevens, for their own gifts as writers and for their steady, unwavering love and support.

Also I wish to express my fondness and gratitude to Binky Urban and Sloan Harris at ICM, and to Dawn Seferian at Viking, for their kindness, belief, and hard work.

And most especially to my loving husband, Sandy Neubauer, thank you.

Angel
Angel

Augusta

When I was seventeen and beginning to wonder what I was going to do with my life, I started dreaming about angels. Night after night they would come to me softly, so softly that I could never quite see their faces. But when they turned to go I would see their wings. And in the mornings when I'd sit on the side of my bed staring down at my two long white feet, it was remembering those wings, transparent like a dragonfly's and quivering slightly, that made me start thinking of religion.

It was around this time that I decided without ever telling anyone that I wanted to become a nun.

There weren't any nuns in the town where I lived, so I didn't get to see one very often. But that summer, on my way up to Evanston to visit my cousins Camille and Ray, one sat down beside me on the bus. I couldn't believe it. The billowing black fabric, the dangling cross that moved back and forth as she came down the aisle. When the nun chose the empty seat next to mine, I felt a brief dizziness pass over me and I couldn't help taking it as a kind of sign.

She gathered her habit neatly around her in the seat, clasped her hands on her lap, and immediately fell into a deep sleep. I then spent the entire hour before I arrived in Evanston studying the sleeping nun. I looked at the tiny blue veins that branched across her eyelids and at her clean white tightly knit fingers. I even found the courage to reach out and gently touch the black fabric of her habit, deciding for myself that it was made of wool.

By the time the bus rolled into the depot in Evanston, I was more determined than ever about becoming a nun. It was my calling and I could feel it in my blood.

Exactly two days later when my cousin Ray walked into the living room with his friend Gordie Iris, I looked up from the book I was reading and changed my mind.

Part
One

Chapter 1

I'm the one who ended up packing Gordie's things. Not out of anger or wanting never to see him again but because he'd made a mess out of everything and I was accustomed to cleaning up after people. I'd find him sitting out in his studio in front of an unfinished canvas, just sitting there staring into the air, and I'd stand next to him with my hand on his shoulder and tell him that the world wasn't going to end. It just won't end, Gordie, I'd say to him. Or I'd find him at three a.m. down in the living room sitting in the dark and I'd snap on the light and tell him to go to bed. He'd stand without saying a word and slowly walk upstairs. I knew he was thinking about Marion White. In May he'd told me he'd had an affair with her but that he'd ended it. Not long after that he went to pieces.

Finally, after a month had passed and there was no apparent improvement in the situation, I simply took it into my own hands and packed his things. It took me only part of an afternoon since I packed as if he were going off on some business trip for a few weeks, making sure he had enough underwear, getting his shaving things together, his little alarm clock, the book he was in the middle of reading. I packed light, the way he prefers, and when I was pretty sure I'd finished, I zipped up his one small bag and carried it out into the hallway in front of our bedroom and placed it on the rug.

The whole time I'd been packing, Gordie had been sitting in our son Henry's room. Just sitting there on the side of Henry's unmade bed, holding his head in his hands like a basketball. I went and stood in the doorway and softly said, "Gordie," and he shook his head as if I'd asked a question.

"I've got your things all set," I told him. He didn't move. He was looking down at his shoes.

"Gordie," I said, this time a little louder, "before Henry comes home." Then I turned and went back into the bedroom.

I shut the bedroom door and sat down at my little desk where I do the bills and write letters. I heard him come out of Henry's room, pick up the suitcase, and go down the stairs. A second later the screen door on the porch slammed shut and I got up and looked out the window. I watched him come across the lawn and open the trunk of his car. He threw the suitcase in. Then he just stood there for a long minute staring at it. I sighed. I had the feeling he wasn't going to go. But he finally reached and shut the trunk and got into the car. A second later the sound of the engine bloomed up and a second after that he was gone. God only knows what was going through my mind, but I went over and straightened the clips in my hair, then went downstairs and started dinner.

That first week after he'd left, I couldn't help feeling the way I used to when I'd sent the boys off to their grandparents in Illinois. It was a combination of relief and emptiness, a feeling that time suddenly appeared in front of me, looking me in the face. I organized my days, getting to things I'd been putting off for months, cleaning my car, the downstairs hall closet, weeding the entire vegetable garden. Of course, there were moments where Gordie's absence struck me so hard I'd get the feeling I was going to go out from underneath myself. But I learned how to get through them simply by putting a thought inside my head and leaning towards it. I'd think, Henry's out of socks, and before long I'd be down in the basement filling the washing machine, humming a little louder than usual to myself.

The night of what should have been his graduation, after eating dinner in the kitchen with his mother, Henry borrowed her car and drove up to the high school parking lot. He'd intended to go in and watch the ceremony, but he wound up lying on the hood of the car smoking a joint, then staring up at the stars. His father had been gone a week but still the thought of it, of him living someplace else, with someone else, circled around Henry's head like a small trapped bird, fluttering, crashing around, never quite coming to rest.

The parking lot was dead quiet, just the hum of the big lights and occasionally a faint round of applause sounding from inside. By the time the herd of graduates came pouring out through the doors in their caps and gowns, popping open champagne bottles and whooping with joy, he'd lost himself so completely to the pot and the constellations that it took him a minute to figure out what was going on. He sat up and rubbed his face and stared straight ahead; then he got back in his car and followed the long slow snake of cars to the graduation party.

At the Hillens' house, where the party was, they'd put up a tent and someone had strung little lights everywhere. Henry parked on the side of the road and walked across the lawn. When he arrived at the tent someone shouted, "Hey Henry, wasn't the same without you. Maybe next year, huh?" All night long people kept slapping him on the back, telling him they were going to miss him. It gave him a caved-in kind of feeling at first, but after he had a few beers the feeling went off.

He wound up sitting cross-legged next to the keg, filling and re-filling his big plastic cup with beer. Some people had him sign their yearbooks. He'd find the page with his picture and name (when they made the book they hadn't realized he wouldn't be graduating) and he'd sign, "Good times and bad times and lots of them. Henry Iris." He'd sign his signature in a big looping way, so that his hand flew off the paper when he finished. He was getting too drunk to think of anything else to say. He even signed his old girlfriend's book that way. She read it and gave him a bewildered look. "Christ, Henry, thanks a lot," she said and walked away.

By midnight the party was in full swing and he was still sitting next to the keg. Just when he started to realize how drunk he was getting, he noticed a girl standing alone in front of him, leaning against one of the tent poles, looking out at the dancers.

"Hey," he said.

She turned and looked at him flatly, then went back to watching the dancers.

"Hey bird face," he said. "Hey, come here and talk to me."

"What'd you call me?" She turned back towards him, frowning.

"Bird face," he said, grinning up at her. She had long whitish blond hair and eyes the color of robin's eggs. He couldn't remember ever seeing her before.

She pointed at herself. "You called me bird face?"

"Yup."

"Is that some sort of come-on?" She looked mildly disgusted.

"Highest compliment," he said, "coming from a bird lover like myself."

"Huh." She squinted down at him for minute, then turned and walked off through the dancers, her thin arms swinging like two pieces of rope.

He watched her go, then stood up and filled his empty cup with beer; then, after standing for a minute thinking, he climbed up on top of a metal folding chair and yelled, "Hey!" Everybody turned and looked at him. "Hey," he called again, this time holding up his cup of beer. "Good luck, suckers!" And dumped the beer over his own head.

People went crazy laughing and shouting, *"Hen-ry! Hen-ry!"* He stood there dripping with beer and grinning; then he took a deep drunken bow and got down off the chair. He'd known half of them since kindergarten.

After that he walked out across the lawn. He was singing his favorite Bob Dylan song, "Mr. Tambourine Man." When he reached the far edge of the lawn he looked back and squinted his eyes so that all the little lights strung up around the tent became blurred. He stopped singing and stood still and for a minute imagined himself just walking into the woods and disappearing, walking clean out of his own life. He imagined how people would describe him for years afterwards as the guy who dumped beer all over himself and then vanished off the face of the earth. He thought about his father getting the news, and the girl with the bird face getting the news.

But after a while he started singing again. "Hey Mr. Tambourine man play a song for me, in the early morning hours I come follllowing you." He turned around and walked into the woods, the trees looming up around him in the dark.

As it turned out, he was the last one to leave the graduation party. He had fallen asleep in the woods and woken up to the sun coming through the trees. He was lying on his back and he looked up at the thousands of green shimmering leaves above him before standing. It was so quiet that he could hear the grass brushing against his sneakers as he started walking across the lawn. He was no longer drunk. His mind felt as clear as the Hillens' blue swimming pool. Last one to go, he thought to himself as he walked through the tent kicking at the empty plastic cups on the ground, how appropriate.

When he climbed the stairs at six-thirty that morning, his mother came out of her bedroom. She hadn't cried once about his father as far as Henry could tell. But there was something seized up about her that he'd never seen before. "What have you been up to?" she said, tilting her head slightly to the side and giving him a sad, loving look.

He glanced down at his clothes; they were dirty from lying on the ground and there were still leaves stuck to the back of his hair. "I fell asleep in the woods."

"Well, I hope the whole thing wasn't too depressing, honey," she said.

Henry shrugged.

His room was flooded with sunlight when he lay down on his bed. He suddenly felt too tired even to take off his sneakers so he let them hang off the end of the mattress. He heard his mother tiptoe down the stairs and, with every soft step, he suddenly swore he felt her pain through his own limbs. He closed his eyes.

Not long after that he fell into a heavy sleep and had a dream that the bird-faced girl from the party was walking ahead of him up a wooded trail. He could see her tan arms swinging and her hair pouring off her head like milk as she moved up through the saplings. He was trying to catch up to her but the long blue graduation gown he was wearing kept catching on branches and stones, billowing out behind him like a big blue cloud, and keeping him just a few steps out of reach of that small graceful body.

That Saturday morning, after Henry stumbled in from his party, without fully realizing it, I made a grocery list that resembled the ones people make who are preparing for wars or blizzards. It covered two eight-by-ten pieces of lined paper and had things like canned soups and frozen dinners on it. After sitting alone down in the kitchen I went back upstairs and got dressed. I wore a white button-down shirt, a khaki skirt with snaps up the front, and a pair of sandals. I combed my hair, which was looking a little out of control, pinned it back with two bobby pins, and pinched my cheeks for some color.

Before going back downstairs I stood for a minute in the doorway of Henry's room and looked in at him. He was sleeping on his back with his mouth wide open and his breath coming and going steady as a clock. His room smelled of old beer and cigarettes and his clothing lay in piles around the floor. I felt like walking over to him, touching his forehead, pulling down the blinds, unlacing his sneakers. Instead I walked down the stairs, holding my pocketbook in my left hand and trailing my right one along the banister.

When I walked into the store that morning, right off I knew that I was news. It wasn't that anyone said anything, it was just that they all took a good look at me. Their eyes dug into my face and searched around for some sign of distress. I smiled and said hello to the people I knew but I concentrated on my shopping. I held my list in one hand, pushed my cart with the other, and scanned the shelves carefully with my eyes. My sandals made a soft thwopping sound against the bottoms of my feet and the junky music played delicately over the speakers.

By the time I reached the fourth aisle my cart was so full that I had to go back up front and get another one, leaving the first by the checkout counter. As I was rounding the corner into the fifth aisle I heard a voice say, "How are you, dear?"

I turned around and saw Doris Breer, an older woman whom I have known for years through the library. She was looking up at me. "Augusta, are you all right?" she asked.

I pointed at myself. "Me? Why wouldn't I be?" I laughed a little.

But Doris didn't seem the least bit convinced. "Do you need anything, dear?" she said. "I'm happy to help you out anytime you need anything."

I kept my baffled look and said, "Well, Doris, I'm not quite sure I understand, but of course, thank you."

I turned and walked quickly down the aisle, forgetting to look at my list, forgetting to even look on the shelves. I turned the corner and stopped and stood there for a minute. I was breathing quickly, as if I'd had the wind knocked out of me. A young girl was standing nearby with a baby and the baby was looking at me.

"Halloo," I whispered. "Halloo sweetie."

"Oh, wow," the girl said. "You wouldn't mind holding him for a second, would you? I got to go get one of those big things of dog food and he won't stay in the cart."

I reached out my arms and the girl handed me the baby. "Thanks a lot, I'll be right back," she said.

I stood there holding the baby in my arms while the girl rushed down the aisle and disappeared around the corner. His downy head brushed against my cheek and I raised my hand up and smoothed my palm over his soft skull. I hadn't held a baby in so long. The compact little body, skin as smooth as a pearl, that smell of powder and baby food. I leaned my head towards him and hugged him. He squirmed for a minute, then gave in, relaxing in my arms. I suddenly had a powerful desire to run with him. I actually imagined myself stealing that baby, running out of the store, plopping him in my car and driving off.

"Hey lady, are you okay?" The girl was standing in front of me, staring into my face. "You all right?"

I nodded and handed her back the baby. I was smiling but there were tears running down my cheeks. "You sure you're all right? Maybe you should call somebody or something?" the girl said.

I shook my head and opened my pocketbook. I dug around for a minute and found a tissue and wiped my face. The baby was reaching his hand out towards me. "Bye-bye, precious," I whispered.

The girl was leaning on one leg looking at me.

"You like kids, don't you?" she said.

"Yes, I do."

"Well, anytime you want to baby-sit or anything, hey, no problem."

"Thank you," I said, and I turned and walked slowly out of the store, leaving my two full carts and my grocery list behind. I walked out across the parking lot with the summer pushing up against me like a thick wall and slid into my hot car and shut the door. "Oh God," I heard myself say and I lay down across the front seat. I brought my hands up and cupped them over my face and the darkness felt so good I just kept them there.

It could have been a minute later or three hours. I'd lost track of time when I heard Henry yelling, "Mom! Are you okay?" I pulled my hands away from my face and looked up at him. He was standing with the car door open, panting. His face was white like milk.

"Are you okay, Mom?" he said. This time he was pleading with me.

I began to answer but then I lost the words. They just left my mind and I stared down at the floor of the car.

"They were going to call an ambulance. Jesus Christ. Hang on."

He slammed the door and I heard him outside the car talking. He was saying, "She's just not feeling well but she'll be okay. . . ."

At this point another voice, the voice of a man, was saying something.

"No, really," Henry said. "No, I'm just going to take her home, she'll be okay."

Henry opened the door and said, "Mom, if you don't sit up they're going to call an ambulance, now sit up."

It was an order and I didn't have to think about it so I sat up. I sat up but I kept my eyes lowered to the floor. There were people looking at me, I felt that, but I refused to see them.

Henry ran around the outside of the car, opened the trunk, and I heard him throw in his bicycle. He then got back in the car, rolled down the window and said, "Thanks a lot," and started the car.

"Jesus," he kept muttering frantically as he drove home. "Jesus Christ."

It was nighttime when I woke up in my bed. My eyes simply flicked open and I looked around, for a second confused about what time it was. I didn't see Henry sitting there in the corner at first. He was reading the paper, using a flashlight and moving slowly along the page. He had the paper in front of his face so he didn't see me wake up. But I saw him, his basketball sneakers caked with mud, and the grabbing smell of old beer coming from him. Before I closed my eyes again, I saw that he'd put a little vase on my night table with one yellow marigold from the garden stuck in it. I was thinking now about Gordie. I was feeling inside my body that he wasn't coming back. All up and down my blood I was knowing it.

She'd been lying in bed for three days. Just lying there looking at nothing, barely speaking to him. Henry felt hollowed out from it. Even when he wasn't in the room with her he couldn't shake it. He'd make her cups of tea and pieces of toast and he'd set them down on the table next to her bed and a few hours later they'd still be there.

She would get up in the middle of the night and go down to the kitchen and in the mornings he'd find entire bowls of cereal absorbed in milk or pieces of toast with a single bite taken out of them.

The whole thing felt awkward. She had never even admitted to having a cold before. He found it hard to think of things to say. He'd sit in the chair in the corner of her room and rub his hands across the tops of his legs.

"Don't you want to eat anything, Mom?"

"I'm okay, honey," she'd say, not looking at him. Her voice had gone a little thinner, more like a girl's voice.

"But you haven't eaten much."

"I'm not too hungry, Henry."

After a while he'd stand and walk slowly out of the room. He'd leave the door open but usually the next time he'd pass by, it would be shut again.

He didn't even know how to get hold of his father. He wanted to call him up and tell him she was in bad shape. Other than him he couldn't think of anyone to call. It was surprising; he'd always thought she had a lot of friends, but when it came down to it he couldn't think of one person she'd want to see.

He finally called his brother for lack of any better idea. He realized as he was dialing the number from his mother's address book that he'd never called him before. His brother answered the phone suspiciously—"Hello?"—as if the thing had never rung before.

"Mathew?" Henry said.

"Who is this?"

"It's Henry."

"Henry? Oh. How are you, Henry?"

"Welp. Uh, actually I've sort of been better. There's some stuff going on here?"

"Stuff?"

"Welp, Dad's sort of left. I mean he's been kind of seeing this lady and a few days ago, more like a week actually, he left. And Mom sort of had a kind of breakdown or something."

There was a pause. "Henry, what are you talking about? What do you mean Dad left, where'd he go?"

"I mean he left, I guess he's with this woman."

Another pause, then, in a lowered voice, "What are you saying?"

"Jesus, Mathew, I'm saying it. He left Mom for somebody else."

There was silence on the other end of the phone.

"Anyway, she's not in great shape. She's in bed. I mean she's not dying or anything. She's probably just really upset or something."

When he got off the phone, he was wishing he hadn't made the call. His brother had never been a big part of the family. The news had just seemed to confuse him more than anything.

That night, after getting high out on the lawn, Henry made himself an entire box of frozen waffles for dinner. He sat down in the kitchen and shoveled them into his mouth and looked out at the lawn. It was just starting to get dark out, the trees going black. He heard himself chewing. His fork scraping the syrup on the plate.

Then he stood up, washed his dish, turned off the lights in the kitchen, walked upstairs, and knocked on her door. After a few seconds he pushed it open and stuck his head in the room. "Mom?" he said. " 'Night."

But no sound came out of the dark. Not the sound of her breath. Not her eyes blinking. Not even her head turning to look at him there.

I'd wake up with whole sections of myself floating off in other lifetimes. I'd open my eyes and think I was a girl again, up in my room with my mother downstairs ironing my blouses. Or I'd think Mathew was across the hall in his bassinet. It would take minutes for things to come back together. I'd look around the room, the afternoon light coming through the window, the photographs of Henry and Mathew and Gordie on the bureau, the house dead quiet around me, and there I'd be.

I started remembering things that I'd forgotten about years ago, my mind sparking details one after another. I'd remember the sound of the furnace turning on in the basement of my old house, the heavy rumbling causing the pans hanging in the kitchen to shiver. I'd remember the blue floral pattern on Henry's old rattle. The black beret with the red lettering that Gordie had worn the first time I met him in my cousins' living room. It was easy looking back. I could do it all day, my mind like an old buried landfill.

It was peering into the next second that brought me to a halt. I couldn't do it. Thinking forward gave me a hollowed-out belly where hurricanes took place. I couldn't even get myself into the bathroom without massive indecision, hedging back and forth until my body would finally force me out of the bed.

The only time I felt able to get up was in the middle of the night. Things didn't feel as real at three and four in the morning. I'd go down to the kitchen and try to eat something even though my appetite had deserted me. I'd just sit there and chew and listen to the moths bumping their soft bodies up against the screen door. Then I'd go back through the darkened living room, trailing my hand along the couch and chairs, feeling grateful not to have to see it all—the rugs, the paintings, the lamps.

If someone had actually asked me if I missed him, I'm not so sure I would have said yes. Missing him took the longest time of all to come. It was as if I'd been dropped down onto some other world, where my history, my language, my way of thinking, all were of no use. I was used to Gordie. I'd molded myself around him like a barnacle to the bottom of a boat. Like a piece of machinery that needed him there to keep functioning and now that he wasn't around I'd come to a grinding, awful halt.

I would lie in my bed and hear the cars going by on the road and the neighbors mowing their lawns. I'd smell barbecues, hear the phone ring. I'd just look down over my big-boned body tenting up the sheet that covered me and feel nothing. It wasn't that I couldn't be part of it all. It wasn't that I couldn't rise out of that bed like any strong-willed woman would and push through, it was simply that I had no desire to. There wasn't a hair on my body that felt like joining in, not a breath, not a drop of my blood that wanted to ever be standing in front of the frozen food section of the IGA again. What else can I say? That part of me was gone like a sawed-off limb. Gone. Gone. Gone.

It was Henry who bore the brunt of it too. He'd stand in the doorway and say, "Mom?" His voice had taken on this soft pleading. And if I looked over at his face it would scare me and that fear simply drove me deeper into my state of nothingness. I couldn't take it on. I'd simply look up at the ceiling and say, "I'm okay, honey." But I knew those words were as empty as jars, lidded and transparent. I'd lie there and wait, one, two, three, until he'd turn and go, his footsteps as slow and sad as old Eeyore's.

Chapter 2

Even before his brother called him, Mathew had been mulling over going home. This was because he hadn't been feeling well for some time now. Not in any specific way but more in general terms. He'd been having trouble sleeping and for the first time in his life he couldn't seem to concentrate on his work. He'd sit in his dim little apartment leaning over his stack of note-filled legal pads and ten minutes later he'd find himself in the bathroom studying a patch of dry skin on the back of his arm or trying to decide if he'd always had the two bluish half-moons of dark cupping his eyes.

He'd sworn off just about everything there was to swear off. Red meat and antiperspirants and air conditioners and alcohol (even though he'd never been much of a drinker to begin with). Nothing seemed to help.

So he let the call from Henry be the deciding factor. He'd go home for the summer to recuperate even though he wasn't sure what from. He spent the next several days extracting himself from his life in

Boston. Subletting his apartment. Dropping the one summer course he was enrolled in. He was on the tail end of receiving his Ph.D. in chemistry and it wasn't exactly the best time to leave. But he packed up his car and drove home to Connecticut. He wasn't sure why. It wasn't something he'd normally do. But he drove home anyway.

Six years ago when he'd gone off to Harvard, it hadn't been a big adjustment for anyone. Not for the rest of his family, who had barely seen him when he was home, and not for Mathew, who had managed to live in the house more or less alone all those years.

When he was young, he came home from school every afternoon and went directly to his bedroom and shut the door. He spent his time right up until dinner doing his homework, then taking apart his radio and putting it back together or making a telescope from a kit his parents had given him or just lying across his bed so engrossed in some astronomy book that his mother could call and call from the bottom of the stairs that dinner was ready and he wouldn't even hear her.

His family, though he cared about them, had distracted him more than anything. Made too much noise. Asked him too many questions.

So when he turned into the driveway that afternoon in June and shut his engine off, looking through the windshield at the large looming Victorian house where he had grown up, he felt little but a brief flutter of relief to have the drive over with.

He climbed out of the car, did a few quick yoga moves to loosen the muscles in his shoulders and neck, then began unloading his few belongings.

What he first noticed when he walked into the house was the ashtray on the kitchen table with a mound of cigarette butts rising out of it. The second thing he noticed was how quiet the place was. "Mom?"

he said, standing in the kitchen holding his bags. Nothing. He walked through the house and up the stairs. Her door was shut. He stopped in front of it for a moment. Then he turned and carried his bags into his room and went back down and outside for the rest of his stuff. He'd never seen her door closed like that, in the middle of the day.

After he'd brought everything inside and had a glass of water in the kitchen, he walked back upstairs and stood outside her door. "Mom?" he said again and knocked lightly. Not a sound. He opened the door and stepped into the room. She was sitting up on her elbows in the dim light, squinting towards him. "Gordie?" he heard her whisper, in a plummeting voice so riddled with disappointment that he had the strange sensation he might sink with it right down through the floor.

I thought he was Gordie. When I heard someone lugging stuff upstairs and going in and out of the kitchen door, I just thought he was back. I thought it in the way my mother used to lock the dead bolt on the downstairs doors at night. With a clean flip of my mind, and a thwack, with not a particle of doubt allowed in.

What surprised me was how relieved I felt. I felt so relieved that suddenly I was even taking bigger breaths, as if concrete blocks had been lifted off my chest and I could feel my entire rib cage opening up again. I just hadn't quite realized how much I wanted him back. I hadn't allowed myself to think.

When I heard him moving his stuff into Mathew's room, I assumed he'd decided we shouldn't sleep in the same room for a while. This didn't bother me. Nothing bothered me. I was myself again. I was back to being Augusta Iris, Gordie Iris's wife.

When he finally came into the room, knocking timidly, then swinging the door open, I let my eyes travel over to him in their own time. I wasn't in a rush. When I finally did see him and it wasn't Gordie at all but Mathew, I struggled for a second to realize what was happening. My mind didn't want to take it in, and I called out to him, just called out to him like I was hoping he might hear me wherever he was, before I said, "Oh, Mathew."

Henry was down the road in the cemetery, smoking a joint, leaning against one of the headstones. Even the boneyard felt more cheerful than his house. He'd spent the last week fending off people who'd heard about his mother having a breakdown in the supermarket parking lot. Floods of phone calls from ladies from the church and the garden club and the library and several people who had taken it upon themselves to drive up to the house and knock on the door. Two ladies even showed up with casseroles as if someone had died.

"What do you want me to tell everyone, Mom?" he'd asked from the doorway of her bedroom.

"I really don't care," she'd whispered, keeping her head turned away from him. "Tell them whatever you want."

So he started to tell them she was away on a trip.

"A trip?" The response was surprise.

"Yeah, she's on a hiking trip," he heard himself say. "Out in Yosemite National Park." He'd seen a show that week on TV about Yosemite, that's where he'd come up with it.

"I had no idea your mother was a hiker, Henry."

"Yup. She's always done a lot of hiking." He wasn't sure he sounded convincing. Or why he was even covering for her, for that matter.

Finally he went around the house that morning and unplugged all but the one phone in the living room. That way, most of the time, he wouldn't even hear it ringing. Then he walked down to the cemetery. He sat with his back up against a headstone and smoked his joint and looked out in front of him. It had turned to summer without his even realizing it. Everything gone lush and tangled. The past couple of weeks had been seasonless in the house, as if time had come to a screeching stop and nothing like weather seemed to matter.

He sat for close to an hour in the sun, leaning his head back against the old headstone. He realized he was hoping that when he got back to the house his father's car would be sitting in the driveway as it always was. Not that he missed his dad exactly. But he felt scared for his mother. As if there were a snake hole of fear winding down through his stomach.

As he was walking out of the cemetery Jeff Truly pulled up alongside of the road in his truck with his flatbed of lawn mowers in tow.

"Hey Dr. Iris!" he yelled. Henry knew Jeff from having bought pot from him the past few years. He had a lawn-mowing business during the summer and sold a little pot in the winter months.

"Hey," Henry said and walked over to Jeff's truck.

"Hey listen, you want a job? This fucking kid just left me high and dry!" Jeff had shut his engine off but was still shouting above it.

"Uh, I don't know," Henry said. "I kind've got some stuff going on."

"Twelve bucks an hour and a tan." Jeff got out of the truck. He was wearing nothing but shorts and work boots.

"Twelve bucks an hour?"

"Yup. I'm desperate. I'm already backed up three days."

"Jesus," Henry said. He was still stoned and his mind was a little weighty.

"What the hell else are you doing this summer?"

Henry scratched the top of his head. "Not a whole lot."

He wound up mowing half the cemetery lawn for Jeff as an experiment, during which he decided to take the job. He figured it would be good to have an excuse to get out of the house. Plus, he could use the money towards buying a car in the fall.

When he got home late that afternoon, his sneakers covered with cut grass and his hands smelling of gasoline, he found his brother's car sitting in the driveway and he heard himself say, "Awh, crap," just at the sight of it.

Seeing her in bed in the middle of the day gave Mathew the shakes. He stood in her dark room and felt his knees start to waver at the image of her lying there motionless under the sheets. "Mom?" he almost hollered. "What's the matter?"

She didn't answer right off. There was a frightening pause before she spoke; then finally all she said was, "Oh Mathew," and her voice came out crippled; it was thin and bent and dark as the room.

It was a shock. Even though Henry told him she was in bed, he hadn't expected it. He stood there with his two hands hanging down at his sides and was unable to think of anything to say. All he knew was that he suddenly felt weak. Like he might collapse. He heard her sniffle. He realized she was crying. "Mom," he said, his voice part of his breath.

"I thought you were Gordie," she wept. "I'm sorry, honey, I thought you were him." She rolled over into her pillow.

It was as if he'd seen a picture of her naked. That's how it made him feel. Awkward. Unable to think.

Finally, he just backed out of the room and shut the door again. He stood in the hallway and touched the wall with his hand. He felt dizzy, as if he'd just taken a large blow to the head. He turned and slowly went down the stairs.

When he walked into the kitchen, his brother was standing by the sink filling a glass from the faucet. He had hair down to his shoulders and he wore a sagging tee-shirt with the sleeves ripped off. When Henry turned towards him, Mathew saw that the shirt had the word "STONED" printed across it in big black letters.

"Hey, how are you?" Henry said.

Mathew put his hands on the counter and looked at him. He shook his head. "She's in her room crying."

"I know."

"What happened, Henry? I mean, is she sick or something?" His voice came out sounding desperate.

"I told you on the phone. No, she's not sick. She's heartbroke . . . or whatever you call it." Henry turned and drank the glass of water.

Mathew just stood there. He was still shaking his head. His stomach was turning. "I can't believe this," he said.

"Yeah, well," Henry muttered, "I sort of couldn't believe it either. But . . ." He looked at Mathew and shrugged. "Anyway, I got to take a shower."

After Henry left, Mathew stood for a long time looking down at his hands on the counter. He felt as if all his blood had left him when he'd seen her lying there. It shocked him. Truly shocked him. She'd always driven him crazy, hovered over him, cooked him too much food, talked incessantly.

Now he stood in the kitchen and tried to think what to do. He was at a loss. Go back in and talk to her? She didn't seem to want it. Make himself something to eat? He hadn't eaten all day but the thought of food made his stomach quiver. So he turned and walked slowly through the house and up the stairs and past her door. He walked into his room and stood for a minute looking at nothing; then he lay down across the bed with his shoes still on and stared up at the ceiling.

He lay for a long time, not moving, just his heart banging inside his chest. He didn't move until the sun was down and his room was pitch-black; then he got up and went back across the hall and knocked timidly on her door. After getting no response, he gently pushed it open.

I had no idea what time it was when I woke up to him standing there in the middle of the room. But it was dark and I heard him saying, "Mom?" Like he wasn't sure it was me lying there in the bed. I turned and I could just see the outline of him against the hallway light. Rail thin and stooped at the head from spending his life reading book upon book.

Unlike Henry, who came into the world bumping his head, screaming bloody murder, needing Band-Aids left and right, Mathew came into it silently, needing close to nothing. A tiny pale baby with long fingers, he barely cried and never smiled. He'd wake from his naps and lie there in his crib staring up at the mobile that hung from the ceiling. I'd walk into the room waving, making silly noises, and he'd glance over at me, then go back to watching the slow floating fishes and swans.

"Yes, Mathew," I said from under the covers.

He stood there for a long moment and I thought I saw him wavering slightly, like he was on the bow of a rocking boat. Then he turned and went out of the room closing the door behind him.

I think he thought I was dead.

Chapter 3

They'd mowed only two lawns when the rain started. At first it was just a sprinkle, slowly covering the windshield of Jeff Truly's truck, but within half an hour it began to come down hard and straight. They parked on the side of Hutchins Road and smoked a joint and listened to Jeff's Muddy Waters tape. Henry was beginning to realize that since he'd started the job he was smoking a lot more. There were moments during the day when he would try to remember the last time he wasn't stoned and his mind would stretch and search and usually come up empty.

But Henry loved mowing the lawns. He loved leaning down and yanking the starter cord and hearing the engine roar up around him. It made the rest of the world peel away and he'd pace for hours back and forth across the grass. He found he could think more clearly while he was mowing. He could organize his head in a way he couldn't when he was just lying on his bed at home. He could put things in perspective so that when he snapped the loud motor off and the summer rushed back at him, he would feel different, as if he'd just gotten off a plane from some far-off place and everything that was familiar to him looked sharp and new.

"Welp," Jeff said, leaning his head out into the rain and looking up at the sky. "That's that."

Henry was staring at the drops of rain on the windshield, the way they hit hard and rolled down, hundreds every second.

Jeff pulled his dripping head back into the truck and looked over at Henry. "Where to, bonehead?"

Henry shrugged. "Home I guess, back to the morgue."

Jeff bent forward and started the truck and they pulled out onto the road.

When they were almost home, Henry changed his mind and told Jeff to drop him off down at the supermarket. The idea of being in the house all day filled him with dread.

They drove through town slowly, the way Jeff always drove when he was stoned, slow and cautious and using his blinker for a good eighth of a mile before he made his turns. At one point Henry looked behind them and saw a long line of cars, all with their lights and their windshield wipers on. It reminded him of a funeral procession. Like they were about to bury the two tarp-covered lawn mowers that were in the back of the truck. He imagined everyone in black standing around dabbing at their eyes as he and Jeff shoveled dirt onto the mowers.

After Jeff dropped him off in front of Merly's IGA, Henry went in and got a cup of coffee from the deli counter. Then he sat down on one of the benches in front and watched the rain pour across the parking lot. He sat under a corrugated metal overhang and when the rain came down heavy it sounded like machine gun fire above him. He stayed there and smoked one cigarette after another. People would get out of their cars and come tearing across the parking lot, kids screaming, their mothers trying to run behind them, holding some lame piece of paper over their hair.

He must have been there for close to an hour when a white Nova that sounded like it had dropped its muffler pulled into the lot and parked out at a far corner. He wouldn't have even noticed it if the girl who got out hadn't come walking casually across the pavement through the pouring rain. Not in the least bit of a rush.

She walked up to him and stopped in front of the bench.

It was the girl from the graduation party. Henry hadn't thought of her since that night. He'd been distracted by all the stuff going on with his family, and besides, he figured he'd just been drunk. But now looking up at her, he remembered he'd called her bird face.

"Hey," he said. Then he couldn't think of anything to say.

She reached up and tucked her soaking-wet hair behind her ears. She had skin the color of Bit-o-Honey bars and her whitish blond hair seemed to spring off it. "So, is this what you're doing with your summer?" she said.

He shook his head. "Actually, I've been mowing lawns."

"Oh." She looked behind her at the parking lot, the rain coming down so hard that it was bounding off the pavement. "Good day for it, huh?"

"Yeah," Henry said. His mouth had dropped open and he was staring up into her face. He was realizing she wasn't just pretty, it was more that she was hard not to look at. The smoothness of her skin and her big blue eyes.

"Welp," she suddenly said, "see ya round." And she turned and walked into the store, leaving him on the bench feeling stunned.

After a minute he got up and followed her. She was standing in front of the bread section with a cart, her brown legs covered with goose bumps. "Hey, wait a sec."

She turned and looked at him. "Hey what?"

"Hey, I don't know, what are you up to?"

"Well, looks to me like I'm shopping."

He smiled and dug his hands into his pockets. "Jesus, it's subzero in here."

"I know." She turned, grabbed a loaf of bread and threw it into the cart, then pushed down the aisle and stopped in front of the dairy section. Henry followed her. He stood behind her and watched her pick up a half gallon of milk and put it in the cart.

"You know, I don't know what your name is," he said. "I mean, if you told me that night at the party, hate to say it but I was too damn drunk to remember."

"No, I didn't tell you. You had come up with your own name for me, if you recall."

"Yeah, I recall, well, I was sort of drunk."

"Yeah, well, my name is Bette."

"Bette. Bette what?"

"Bette Mack." She turned again and pushed the cart down the aisle, around the corner, and up the next aisle. Henry stayed behind her.

"So *Bette,* don't you want to know who I am?"

She stopped and laughed. "Ha! I know who you are." She was looking over the cereal section, scanning the shelves.

"Oh," he said. He couldn't seem to take his eyes off of her. "I can't believe I never talked to you before. How long have you lived here anyway?"

She shrugged and pushed the cart a little way down the aisle. "We moved here in March." She found a box of raisin bran and heaved it into the cart.

"Where'd you live before?"

She was about to answer but something behind him caught her eye. Right then Henry felt someone touch his shoulder and he turned around and saw his father standing in a raincoat he'd never seen before. "Henry." His voice was strange and hoarse, his hair wet, his glasses slightly fogged up.

Henry couldn't move for a second. He hadn't seen his father once since the day he'd left. Seeing him made everything inside come to a halt. After all, it was his father and he could feel in his blood a kind of relief just to see him. To know he still existed. Yet at the same time, he couldn't bring himself to hug him or even say hello. Finally, after standing there stunned for several more seconds, Henry turned and walked quickly out of the store.

A little while later when Bette climbed into her car, he was sitting there in the passenger seat smoking a cigarette and grinning over at her.

"Hey," he said. "You mind giving me a lift up to my house?"

She made a face, as if she couldn't quite see him through her eyes. Then she leaned forward and started her car.

Mathew lay like a cadaver on his bed in his old room, his hands cupped under his head, his sharp elbows pointing out to the sides like a pair of wings. It had been raining for three days. Hard rains that hammered down on the roof. Rains that made his already dark room darker yet.

He lay with his eyes open and stared blankly up at the ceiling and constantly monitored how he was feeling. And it wasn't well, either. In fact, he was feeling a good deal worse than he had two weeks ago in Boston. He found himself unable to sleep more than a couple of hours now; he'd wake up over and over throughout the night then thrash this way and that in bed trying to get comfortable again. He also found that certain thoughts gave him a flooding of heartbeats, heartbeats that would rise up like thousands of tiny birds lifting into the air. Thinking of his mother lying alone in her room. Thinking of his dim little apartment in Boston, wishing in some ways he'd just stayed there. Even thinking of going down to the kitchen brought on a sudden thumping of his heart.

His room hadn't changed any from when he was growing up. His science books were still arranged in alphabetical order on the shelves, his insect collection was neatly stacked in his closet, his desk drawers still contained dinosaur erasers, chewed pencils, stamps that he had peeled off of letters. His bureau had socks that he'd worn back in seventh grade, a jigsaw puzzle that only he had been able to do, a plastic bag filled with various screws and washers from something—he couldn't remember what—he had taken apart and never put back together.

The room reminded him of a museum of his own history. Like one of those homes of famous people where everything is preserved as it had been when the person was alive. He was constantly remembering himself, seeing himself as he had been growing up. And what he saw made him feel odd, almost nostalgic for those days when he would spend his time alone up in his bedroom, hiding from his loud, ridiculous family, soaking up one book after another.

It was eleven in the morning and the house was dead quiet. Mathew's stomach was calling out for food, moaning and turning over and over. He swung his legs off the side of the bed and slipped his feet into his two worn Chinese slippers. He was wearing a pair of paisley cotton pajamas, another relic of the past that he'd found in his bureau. They were pajamas he remembered wearing in ninth grade. Yellow with green tadpolelike swirls. They were definitely too small, climbing a few inches above his ankles and wrists, but they were worn and thin and, all in all, pretty comfortable.

He shuffled out into the hall and stood for a second listening for some sign of life. After hearing absolutely nothing he got up on his tiptoes and walked over to his mother's door. He placed his ear then the tips of his ten fingers on the wood and held his breath. Not a sound. He stood back and thought for a second, then tapped very gently with the back of his hand. "Mom?" he said quietly. His heart was starting up again and as he listened for some response from inside he could hear the blood rushing through his ears.

He knocked again, this time a little harder. "Mom?" he said.

There was a pause; then he heard the bed creak and the rustle of sheets.

"Mathew?" he heard his mother's voice say. "Come in."

Mathew opened the door and peered into the pitch-black room. It smelled to him of sadness, thick and unyielding, immediately making his head swirl. He could just make out the outline of his mother under the sheets. "Are you okay, Mom?" he said.

"It's raining," she whispered. "Keeps raining."

"I know." He stood there touching the doorway with his hands, waiting for her to say something else.

"Tomorrow's the Fourth," he finally said.

"Fourth?"

"Of July." Mathew's voice sank; he suddenly wondered why he was telling her this. Like she would need to know. "Fourth of July."

He saw her nod. She was lying on her side with her knees tucked up near her stomach. "I'll bring you some tea and something to eat," he said, and after staring in for another minute, he backed out and pulled the door shut again.

Seeing his mother in this condition made him feel so off balance that he had to hold onto the banister while going down the stairs. His legs had taken on a loose feel again.

Henry was sitting in the kitchen eating a large stack of waffles drenched with maple syrup. He was bent over his plate, chewing and reading the comics laid out on the table in front of him.

"Good morning, Henry," Mathew said.

"Hey," Henry said through his chewing, and glanced up at Mathew.

"No lawns today again?"

"Nope." Henry looked back down at the paper.

Mathew stared for a second at the waffles. His mouth was salivating. He hadn't had waffles since he was a kid.

Henry glanced up again. "Want some? There're about twenty boxes in the freezer. I stocked up."

"Thank you," Mathew said. "But no. I try not to eat anything with preservatives."

Henry shrugged and went back to eating.

Mathew stood at the stove and made a bowl of hot millet, then sat down across from Henry and spooned the yellow mush into his mouth.

Henry peered into the bowl and made a face. "Good?"

"It's okay," Mathew said. In fact, it wasn't a flavor he could spend much time defending. It tasted slightly metallic, with a bitter after-taste. But he tried not to think about it.

"I think she's worse," Henry suddenly said after a minute. He was scraping the side of his fork on his plate, moving the leftover syrup around.

Mathew took the spoonful he was about to eat and dropped it back into his bowl. He looked down into the millet. His appetite just van-ished at the mention of his mother.

"I don't know, maybe we should call someone or something," Henry said. "I was thinking maybe we should call that old friend she sometimes talks about. Kate something or other? You know, the old high school friend?"

Mathew shook his head; he didn't have any idea who Henry was talking about. If his mother had ever mentioned an old friend he probably hadn't been listening at the time. He'd had a habit of not listening to her.

"Well, anyway, she sometimes talks about this person Kate. I don't know. I think they used to be friends before Mom got married."

Mathew shrugged. He could feel his stomach pinching at the mil-let. "Maybe," he said, not knowing what else to say to his brother.

Henry stood up and sighed and brought his plate over to the sink.

Mathew looked out the window at the rain coming down across the lawn. The overgrown grass was flattened and there were puddles forming in sunken parts. If it was a physical problem then maybe he could participate. He could figure out a diet for her or a kind of herbal medicine or massage therapy. But it was just sadness that kept her up in bed. Overpowering sadness that leaked right out of her room and into his. It was such sadness that it brought him to a state of paralytic fear. It took hold of him and shook him and after a while he got lost inside it and stopped knowing anymore if it was her sadness or his own, flooding through him like a big dark river that had been dammed and dried up for years.

I dreamed that I was walking alone through some field, through very green grass. Like Ireland. And suddenly the sky filled up with magnificent birds, red and blue and yellow and big like dogs, their wings moving graceful and slow. They passed overhead, and they were all saying, "Well, anyway." Then they were gone. And I woke up.

It was the end of the day. Though as usual there was that moment when I couldn't tell if it was morning or evening, if the day was ahead of me or behind me. Then slowly I figured it out.

I heard Mathew coming up the stairs. It was as if sandpaper were taped to the bottom of his shoes. I heard it a few times a day. *Shhhh-shhhh-shhhh-shhhh.* Tonight he knocked then came shuffling into my room. He was carrying a tray and he put it down on the little table beside my bed. "It's seaweed soup," he said. "Full of nutrients."

I nodded.

He just stood there for a minute, not looking at me, looking at the bowl of soup. His hands hanging there at his sides.

"Are you hungry?" he asked.

"Not too," I told him.

"Well . . ." He looked at the space above my head. "I'll leave it anyway."

He went out. *Shhhh-shhhh.* Shut the door. I lay there for a while and before long I started smelling the soup. Salty and grabbing at my nostrils. Like the ocean. And when I closed my eyes I could see it, that blue-green water going out and coming back.

Not so long after dark I heard the fireworks start. At first I thought it was some kind of gunfire, some war going on; then I remembered the Fourth of July. I got out of bed and went over to the window and pushed the shade to the side. I stood and listened to the big booms and the small rapid popping. They do them up at the school over the big soccer fields. The year before, Gordie hadn't wanted to go. For all I know, he was probably seeing Marion way back then. So I'd gone up alone and spread out an old blanket and sat down on the grass and watched the colors spray down across the sky.

Now, standing by the window, I suddenly pictured myself clearly up there at the school, sitting on my blanket on the grass, my face flickering blue and red and pink from the big explosions in the sky. I saw myself as if I were looking at some photograph of another person. Some lady in her khaki shirt, her comfortable shoes, surrounded by loud tangled families. A lady who sat still while everything inside her felt like it was about to burst open and come sailing down in hundreds of colors. I saw myself having no one there to turn to and just say, "Oh, isn't it glorious."

I heard Mathew come back in the room later on, the sandpaper shuffle that approached the bed and stopped. I knew he was looking at me, a mound under the covers, a big lump that didn't move. But I was grateful not to have to see him, to have the blankets pulled right up over my head and the darkness holding on to me like a sponge.

Every shirt Henry owned stank of B.O. There was a mountain of them, in fact, in the middle of his room, and he went through the whole thing smelling the armpits. "Oh man," he kept saying, tossing them into a new reject pile. "Whew."

Finally he went down the hall and knocked on his brother's door. After a minute he heard Mathew's voice. "Yes."

Henry opened the door and walked into the room. The shades on all the windows were pulled down and Mathew was lying on the bed in his pajamas. It was five in the afternoon.

"Mind if I borrow a shirt? Mine are all dirty."

Mathew motioned to his bureau. "Middle drawer, long sleeves on the left, short on the right," he said, then went back to looking up at the ceiling.

Henry walked across the room and opened the drawer. There were four piles of meticulously folded shirts and he noticed right off that half of them were old shirts he himself had worn back in eighth and

ninth grade. Mathew had been wearing Henry's old clothes for a long
time now. Not only was he smaller than Henry but he'd never been
big on keeping up with any fashions.

Henry lifted a red polo shirt off the top of a pile, turned and held
it up for Mathew. "This all right?"

His brother shrugged. "Doesn't matter."

"I'm having a girl over for dinner," Henry said. "Then we're going
to head up to the fireworks."

"Okay." Mathew nodded. "I'll avoid the kitchen."

"You don't have to avoid the kitchen, I don't care. I just thought
I should tell you."

"All right, then." Mathew sounded bored out of his mind.

"Welp." Henry paused before walking out of the room. "Thanks
for the shirt."

"Okay," his brother said and Henry pulled the door shut.

It's like living in a hospital, he thought to himself as he walked
down the hall, passing his mother's closed door and feeling her lying
there too, just lying there, not moving.

Later when Bette Mack came into the kitchen in a cloud of perfume
and banana-flavored gum, the first thing she said was, "So! Where is
everybody? I thought you had a family."

"Ah," Henry said. He was in the throes of making pancakes from
scratch. "Right, well, they're here. Sort of anyway. Is baking soda and
baking powder pretty much the same thing?"

"Nope, I wouldn't say so." Bette dropped her immense shoulder
bag onto the floor, slipped her feet out of her sandals, and plopped
down in a chair. "They're here? But am I going to, like, meet them?"

"Who?" Henry said, looking up from the cookbook.

"Your family."

"Oh, well, no, I sort of doubt it." He let a breath go and leaned against the counter and looked at her. She had on a pair of pink bike shorts and a tight white tee-shirt and her hair was pushed back off her face by a fluorescent pink headband. She was the brightest thing he had seen in months. "My family isn't exactly normal," he said.

"You may continue." She smiled at him. "I'm pure ear."

"Well, it's basically that my father left my mother a few weeks ago and my mother has pretty much been in bed ever since."

"Go on," she said.

"Anyway, my brother seems to be living here now too but he's sort of in the same state my mother's in, don't ask me why. So they're both here, upstairs, and it's highly unlikely you'll see either one of them."

Bette almost looked bored. "Can I smoke?"

"Go for it," Henry said. "I better start these things so we can get up to the fireworks. I was going to make burgers but you said no meat and the only meatless meal I could think of was pancakes. I'm really a lousy cook."

"Don't you have any of those frozen waffles? They're just as good."

Henry dropped the wooden spoon he was holding and gave her a big grin. "You're joking with me, right?"

"Why would I joke with you?" She blew a cloud of cigarette smoke out of her mouth.

He walked over and opened the freezer door and waved a hand in at the dozen boxes of waffles. "A girl after my own heart," he said.

■ ■ ■

Later they drove up in Bette's car to the fireworks. They parked up on
Grail Ridge above the school, beside the Verns' dairy farm, and when
the fireworks started, the cows out in the fields below them began to
bawl nonstop. It was a strange sound, a sort of crazed wailing that
filled the air between all the big booms.

"Look," Bette said, and showed Henry her arms covered with
goose bumps. They were still sitting in her car.

"Is that from the fireworks or the cows?" Henry asked.

Bette said, "Both."

She turned and leaned half her body out the window and looked
down into the fields below. "They must think there's a war going on
or something," he heard her say. Right then another firework whistled
up into the air and blossomed down a red, white, and blue fountain
of color. "Wow," she said, and sat back down in the car and sighed.
"Fireworks sort of flip me out. I know this sounds stupid but they
kind of make me want to cry."

"They make you sad?"

"Not sad, kind of just emotional," Bette said, looking over at him.
"Like the cows."

They both turned to watch another series, this time several small
ones, all different colors that went off one after another. Henry took
the opportunity while she was looking at them to reach out and take
her hand. She let him, not even looking over, just giving him a small
squeeze in return, and right then, from that squeeze, Henry knew
they were together, already, like it had happened without his even
thinking about it. It was a good moment, the best he could remember
in a long time, and yet just as he started to feel that surge of joy he

suddenly pictured his mother lying there in her bed. He saw her eyes, open, blinking in the dark, and he pulled Bette's hand onto his lap, trying to get back into the present, trying to feel that same happiness he'd just started to feel, but somehow, even after she turned to him and they kissed for the first time, it was already gone.

Mathew went to bed at ten o'clock and woke up an hour later feeling as though he'd slept through most of the night. He sat up and snapped on his dim bedside lamp and blinked down into his watch. When he saw the time his heart sank. The thought of another night stretching out in front of him like a bleak desert seemed almost too much to bear.

It was warm and humid out and Mathew's pajama top was clinging to his damp back. He swung his legs over the side of the bed and sat for a minute staring blankly across the room. He'd been dreaming about his father, dreaming he looked out of his bedroom window and saw his father standing on the sidewalk in front of the house. In the dream he'd yelled down, "Dad?" but his father just stood there, hands dug deep into the pockets of his pants, his head tilted slightly to the side as he looked up at Mathew's window.

Now, sitting on the side of his bed, Mathew felt spooked and uneasy. He hadn't spent much time since he'd come home thinking about his father. He'd been too worried about his mother. It occurred to him that his father probably thought he was still in Boston. There was something so unsettling about the thought that Mathew stood up.

He felt he needed air, needed to clear his head. So he stepped into his slippers and shuffled out into the hallway.

The house was pitch-black and dead quiet, like the inside of a casket. Mathew stopped for a second outside his mother's door, holding his breath, listening, before moving past and starting down the stairs. His mind was on the cup of chamomile tea he was planning to make for himself, so he nearly rose out of his body in terror when he heard someone clear his throat in the dark in front of him.

"Jesus!" he said. "Who's that?"

He heard Henry laugh and reached up and felt around the wall for the light switch. When he turned it on, he saw Henry below him on the stairs holding a girl in his arms. She was small, with long blond hair and bracelets covering her right wrist. Both of them were bare-foot.

"Welp." Henry sighed, and set the girl down on her feet. "So much for romantic moments. Bette," he said reluctantly, "this is Mathew."

"Hey," the girl said, suddenly chewing a piece of gum that had been hidden somewhere inside her mouth. "How ya doing?"

Her voice was sharp and piercing. Mathew was so stunned at the sight of her that he just stood there gripping the banister.

"I was wondering when I was going to meet this brother of Henry's," the girl said. "I mean, I kept hearing someone shifting around up here but I was beginning to think it was just some ghost or something."

Henry took her hand and started up the stairs, tugging her along.

"Hey!" she said. "Well, real nice meeting you, Mathew. Sorry about the scare. You know, no offense I hope."

Mathew managed to give his head a slight nod, but his mouth had dropped open and he was staring into the girl's large blue eyes. She stepped past him and followed Henry up the stairs. After Henry's bedroom door clicked shut, he heard her say, "Wow! That's your brother?"

"Yup," Henry muttered. A second later Henry's bed groaned under their weight and Mathew, gaining control of his leg muscles, hurried down the stairs.

His heart was pounding so hard in his chest that he could feel it reverberate throughout his whole body. First being startled like that, then having to stand there in his old pajamas in front of that girl's headlightlike eyes. When he got to the kitchen, he leaned on the counter and took a few large slow breaths. The kitchen stank of cigarette smoke and when he walked over to the wall and flipped on the light, he saw a piled-up ashtray on the table, and underneath one of the chairs a pair of pink canvas sneakers. Mathew looked down at the shoes. They were well worn, with the heels flattened out from being slipped into carelessly. They made him feel as though the girl were still in the room, still staring at him.

He shut off the light, walked back through the living room and out onto the porch. It surprised him that rain was falling lightly through the trees; it somehow cleared his head, hearing it tapping gently.

He sat down on one of the wicker rocking chairs and looked out into the dark of the front lawn. It was difficult for him to stop thinking about his brother with the girl. He'd focus on the sound of the rain or try to remember what his father was wearing in that dream, but in between every thought was the image of Henry upstairs with her.

Mathew only had one girlfriend his whole life. The fall of his junior year in college he'd been partnered in a chemistry lab with a woman who had red hair and large gaps between her front teeth. She'd scared the hell out of him. The way her arm would brush over his when she reached across to get an extra test tube, the way the small hairs on the nape of her neck formed a vee when she wore her hair up. For the first two months there was all that prancing around each other, all those underlying messages, all those awkward moments. Mathew began to have terrible stomach problems. Food moved through him at amazing speeds, entering and leaving his system sometimes within minutes. So when they finally did sleep together, it wasn't that it didn't have its pleasures, but looking back it was more a relief for him to get it over with than anything else.

They stayed together for a few weeks, then over lunch one day came to a mutual agreement that it was costing them both too much time and energy, and that was that. It just ended. Mathew could remember walking out of the coffee shop they had been sitting in and feeling his footsteps lighten as he moved down the street.

Now, sitting on the porch in the rocking chair, he found himself at moments drifting off and waking up a few seconds later still moving back and forth, the bottoms of his feet pushing him gently. It was still raining and the air had taken on the smell of wet earth and grass. His eyes were closed and he finally just let himself drift off into a deeper sleep.

He stayed like that, sound asleep in the chair, until early in the morning. His mouth dropped open and long slow breaths came and went. He probably would have slept the whole night if it hadn't been for Henry's girlfriend's car spinning out of the driveway at a high speed and backfiring right in front of the house so loudly that he flew awake. He thought he'd been shot at first. He thought his heart might blow a large hole through the center of his chest, it was going so hard. He could hear her car roaring down the road, and a few minutes later backfiring again, like a cannon going off. And its echo seemed to go on forever. Echoing through the town and the trees and up across the hills.

Chapter 4

The phone rang all morning long. Just rang and rang like an alarm. Henry had unplugged the one in my room weeks earlier but I could still hear the one down in the living room. It was ringing when I woke up at nine-thirty in the morning. Ringing still when I woke up again at noon. I sat up in my bed and listened to its persistence; then I got up and went out into the hallway and listened to it again. Mathew's bedroom door was shut and Henry's was open but he wasn't around. I stood at the top of the stairs and listened to that phone, going on and on, and I knew it was Gordie. I went down the stairs slowly, holding the banister, walked across the living room, and simply picked it up.

"Hello," he started saying on the other end. "Hello, who's that? Henry? Is that you? Hello?"

"It's not Henry," was all I said, and I heard a breath on the other end—a kind of gasp—then there was a long pause.

"Augusta," he finally whispered. "Oh, I . . . I've been calling all morning."

I didn't say a thing. I just stood there in my pale blue nightgown in the midafternoon sun on our Oriental rug and I squeezed the phone with my hand. I squeezed it as if I were trying to squeeze him right out of it. And his words stopped making sense to me. I didn't hear what he was saying, I just heard the sound of his voice, like an instrument blowing off one long endless note.

I don't know how long I stood there, maybe five minutes or so, before I took the receiver and gently hung it back up, as if I were putting a baby down for a nap. Then I reached around and unplugged the phone. I went over and sat down on the couch and folded my hands in my lap and looked across the room. And the first thing I noticed, not having been downstairs in the daylight for quite some time, was the dust everywhere. A fine white layer that covered every piece of furniture in the room. The very same dust I'd spent twenty-six years chasing around this house. After a bit I leaned forward and touched my finger to the top of the coffee table and wrote the word "goodbye" in the soft layer of white; then I sat back on the couch and just looked at that word for a long time and I knew it was the one word that said everything to me. It was the one word that covered how I felt and what had happened and what was going to happen.

Henry kept muttering it to her. Usually up in his bedroom at night after he slipped all the buttons of her blouse silently out of their buttonholes. He'd whisper, "Where'd you come from, anyway?" It became a kind of running joke with them. She'd give him different answers: "My mother" or "Chicago" or "Work." Even though she knew what he meant. It sometimes just hit him how perfect she was. He hadn't even dreamed of someone like her. Someone that sexy and that much of a companion, too.

She'd come over around eight o'clock every night and they'd sit out on the front porch and smoke cigarettes and talk and watch the cars go by. Then after an hour or so he couldn't stand it anymore and he'd take her hand and pull her upstairs to his room. She wasn't like the other girls he'd slept with, who'd become sort of boneless and limp when they got in bed with him. She was just as eager as he was, a flurry of unbuttoning and unzipping and underwear flying across the room.

He'd been hurling himself at things all his life. The game of baseball, then his set of conga drums when he was thirteen; then it was Bob Dylan and getting high. And with Bette Mack it was the same. He dove right at her. He told her the first time he was with her up in his bed how much he loved her. The words just flew from his mouth like a freed-up bird and took off in a wild uncontrollable flutter into the dark of the room.

Mathew spent his nights up in his bedroom hiding from Henry and his loud girlfriend. He'd eat his dinner early, around five-thirty, then quickly wash his two or three dishes and go up for the night. They were long evenings, and at times he'd ache to go out for a walk, just to get some fresh air, but he never dared. The idea of bumping into his brother and Bette kept him up in his room, doing his yoga or lying around trying to read, eventually going to bed.

Sometimes they'd sit out on the front porch, which was directly underneath his bedroom, and he'd catch whiffs of their cigarette or pot smoke curling up into his window. He'd fan the air with his hand and try not to listen to their conversation but it was a little difficult, her voice being one of those voices that carried. It came right up to him loud and clear, as if she were talking through a megaphone.

"What's that thing you stick into a toilet, you know, what do you call those things that you undo clogs with?" he'd hear her saying.

"Uhm," his brother would sort of grunt.

"Jesus, I can't believe I forgot what they're called. Come on, Henry, what do you call those things?"

"Uh," Henry said.

Mathew wanted to get up off his bed, lean his head out the window, and yell, *"Plunger!"* but he just lay there until his brother finally said, "You mean a plunger?"

"A plunger, exactly, Jesus, I can't believe I forgot what that was called. Anyway, so I needed a plunger this morning at the store and let me just put it this way, I needed it kind of badly. Like major emergency, right? And I called Joel, the store owner, and I'm wild, I said, 'Joel, is there a toilet unplugger-upper thing anywhere in this store?' and he says to me, 'Who's this?' I mean give me a lousy break, he gives me the keys to the store, lets me deal with all his money and he can't even figure out who I am on the phone. I swear the guy must have just smoked a huge joint or something, and to top it off I say, 'It's Bette,' and he goes, 'Bette? Bette who?' I swear I wanted to scream, 'At your store, you idiot!' "

When Mathew realized he was lying there on his bed listening and smiling, he quickly propped himself up on an extra pillow, lifted up his book, and stared into the page.

A few minutes later the book would be back across his stomach and she'd be saying, "I don't know, I think people who travel light are always lonely. I mean seriously, go to an airport sometime and check out all the ones without luggage, they're always alone."

"Huh," Henry would say.

"I think your brother is a light traveler, actually."

"You mean Mathew?"

"Yeah, I mean Mathew, who the hell else is your brother?"

"I don't know."

"I think he falls right into the light-traveler category."

"You think?"

"Well, from the few times I've actually laid eyes on him, I'd say definitely. But now you're the opposite, you're a total overloader."

"Hey!"

"No, that's a good sign. Check out the people who bring too much baggage sometime, they're always the ones having a swell old time. Seriously, I mean maybe they aren't moving at a high speed but they're not unhappy."

"Oh, yeah—well, what about you?"

"Well, I'm a wheel person myself."

"A what?"

"Wheels, I'm into wheels. I've got plenty of luggage but it's all on wheels and it's all organized and I'm moving at a good clip."

Henry laughed. "You're wild, that's what you are."

"Thank you, I take that as a compliment. No, seriously, wheels aren't necessarily a good sign. I mean I tend to move too fast, tend to have things too organized."

"You really are weird."

"Thank you."

There was a long silence. After several seconds it occurred to Mathew, who was still lying on his bed caught up in her words, that they were down there kissing (he'd heard his brother moan), and he quickly leaned over, snapped on his transistor radio, and shoved the earphones into his ears.

The first time I met Bette Mack was at three o'clock in the morning down in the kitchen. I was sitting with the lights off, eating saltine crackers and listening to the mice rustling in the cabinets, when she suddenly appeared in front of me, barefoot and chewing what I later learned was her favorite, a piece of banana-flavored bubble gum.

"Oh my God," I gasped. "Who are you?"

She bit onto her bottom lip and pointed to the ceiling. "I think I'm Henry's new girlfriend. Sorry, I didn't mean to scare you."

"Oh," I said, and brought my hand up over my chest.

"My mother and sister are always telling me I'm scaring the crap out of them 'cause I tend to not make much noise when I walk. Maybe I should get some bells or something and wear them around my ankles."

A second later the overhead light flicked on and she was standing across the room blinking over at me. She said, "Wow, you look so much like Henry ... or I should probably put it the other way around, he looks like you. Unbelievable." She moved across the floor, staring into my face and gnawing on her wad of gum. "Same eyes and mouth, same forehead." She stopped in front of me and reached out her hand. Her arm was covered with silver bracelets that made a soft tinkling sound. "I'm Bette," she said, "and I'm figuring you're Henry's mom."

I nodded and took her hand, which was narrow and tan and wrapped around mine with a surprising squeeze.

"Bette," I said to her. Then I took my hand back and put it in my lap and looked into my palm.

She was standing in front of me and now I could smell her gum and see her feet planted flat and firm on the linoleum floor. I wanted to vanish right about then. I didn't want this girl to think Henry had a mother who looked like this, wearing this old blue nightgown, hair flying in every direction like a witch's. I just sat there and looked into my hands and wished she would go. But she didn't. She stood in front of me and when I finally looked up at her she had her hands on her hips and her head was tilted over to the side and she was looking at me through narrowed eyes.

She shook her head and said, "Henry told me you were having a bad time but I didn't realize it was this bad." Her voice had softened and she reached up into her mouth and took out the gum. She walked over to the garbage and dropped it in, then came back and sat down across the table from me.

"I'm so sorry," I whispered. "I just didn't expect to see anyone."

"Hey!" she said, her voice so sharp that I felt my body jolt from it. "I'm the one who should be sorry, I'm the one who suddenly appears in your kitchen at three in the morning. Don't apologize, Christ, I'm the one who . . ." Her voice trailed off and I looked up and saw that she was pawing through the big leather bag on her lap. After a second she pulled out a pack of cigarettes and a purple lighter, "Mind if I smoke a cigarette?" I shook my head. "Want one?" she asked me. I shook my head again. "Geez, I don't understand how people can get through traumas without cigarettes, in that way they're great inventions."

After she lit it and blew the smoke out she said, "My mom did the complete opposite when my father cut out on her, she went to the other extreme and came out of her shell, you know, started wearing sexy clothes and lots of jewelry and perfume and started listening to all our records. Ugh! It was awful. I mean we just had to sit there and watch her, knowing the whole time that she really was about to lose it. It was the worst. I think you're doing the better thing—you know, just freak out right off and then slowly get better."

I know that my mouth had dropped open at this point and I was just staring into this girl's face.

"I mean, I'll tell you, when my mom finally did hit bottom, well, all I can say is you're looking like Princess Di now compared to what she looked like then."

I shook my head and I reached up and touched my hair, which I knew was in terrible shape. She saw me do this and said, "Hey, wait a sec!" and started digging through her bag again. After a bit she came up with a black velvet headband. "Give this a try, these things can do wonders."

I didn't want to hurt her feelings so I took it and slipped it on over my head. She squinted at me. "Not bad," she said, blowing out another huge amount of smoke from her lungs. "I mean, to be honest, you wouldn't want to show up at the White House with it on but it's not so bad for around here, kind of gives you a tamed look."

"I haven't had the energy to do anything," I told her.

"Don't then, you shouldn't do a damn thing. Just lie as still as you like until the pain checks out. I remember when my mom went through it she used to say it was like getting run over by a bus and having everything broken up in your body. So you just got to let things heal."

I don't know if it was what she was saying or the way she looked or the sound of her voice but whatever it was I began to weep. I heard her start fishing around in her bag again, and a second later she said, "Here." And I looked up and saw her holding a pink tissue out to me in her small delicate hand.

Henry would go in and sit with his mother after work, before Bette came over. He'd sit in the corner and read the classified ads, straining to see in the dim light. She didn't talk. She usually just lay on her back and blinked up at the ceiling and nodded when he told her that it had been a nice day out, or Mrs. Glover, whose lawn they had mowed, had asked about her.

The fact that his father had left was acknowledged around town. This was obvious to Henry. Greg Oliver, the pharmacist, who'd never paid much attention to him before, now made a clear effort to say hello and ask him how things were. "How's your mother, Henry?"

was a question he had to answer several times a day. Never "How's your dad?" It was as if the town had dismissed the very idea of his father.

Sometimes, sitting there in the evening, he'd look up at her and feel certain she was going to die. Die for no other reason than the fact that she was unhappy. This thought made him panic. It made him want to jump up and take hold of her and ask her what the hell she was doing. But he couldn't. It was obvious that this wasn't a choice she'd made. This was something she had no power over. So he'd sit with her for a while then get up and go to the door, glancing once before he pulled it shut behind him, just to see if she was watching him leave; but she'd just be lying still, blank as the walls around her, hardly aware he'd even been there to begin with.

Mathew decided one afternoon after he'd been back home for about three weeks that he'd made a mistake. Coming home to recuperate was not working out. His mind was turning into oatmeal. Every day he was slipping that much farther away from his work and the direction his life had been going for twenty-five years. Enough was enough, he thought after waking up from a long afternoon sleep in his dark room. He wasn't feeling better here—why not go back to Cambridge and at least try to work instead of hiding from Henry's girlfriend all summer?

Thinking this way suddenly seemed to lighten his troubles. He got up off the bed and walked over to the window and took a deep breath. Why hadn't he thought of it before? Being home was all wrong. It had never been a place that had done much for him, why should it be any different for him now?

It was four in the afternoon and he was still in his pajamas, which suddenly struck him as ridiculous. You're letting yourself go to rot, he thought, you should have been changed much earlier in the day. He went over to his bureau and pulled out a fresh pair of underwear and a tee-shirt and a pair of brown cotton trousers and got himself dressed, all the while planning his trip back to Boston. It wouldn't be hard at all. He'd have his job back at the lab in a second, and he'd really get down to work. He ached for a whole day in the library, leaning into his books and notes, letting the world fall away from him.

He finished dressing and he was on his way downstairs to call the lab and let them know he'd be back in a day or two. But as he was passing his mother's door he came to a halt. He stood there for a second listening hard. Then he knocked and said, "Mom?" He opened the door and stepped inside. "Mom?" he said again. She was lying on her side with her back away from him; she didn't answer. He just stood in the doorway, the clock beside her bed ticking loudly. He couldn't think of anything to say, so finally he said, "It's nice out." But she lay still.

After a while he walked out of her room and pulled the door shut. He felt depleted as he went back into his room and lay down on his bed. The thought of leaving seemed absurd now. He knew he wasn't a big help to her. In fact, she'd probably be relieved to have him out of the house rather than lurking around her the way he tended to do. But all the same, without having much reason to stay, he knew he couldn't leave. Couldn't get in his car and just go off. It was no longer possible.

Chapter 5

I knew him so well that I could tell he was awake at night too. Breathing in the sound of all those crickets, just like me. He was sick from what he'd done. Lying beside her without a single hair on his body touching hers. Getting up and going into the bathroom. Looking at his own face in the mirror. I knew him and I knew he was plagued. Wanting to come home and yet at the same time feeling it would kill him to walk back into this house. To be in its grip again. To feel as deadened as he said he had come to feel. Like wood, he told me. He'd gone wooden.

I had listened to him for months telling me everything. We'd go into the bedroom and he would shut the door and tell me he was thinking of leaving. I'd sit there on the chair in the corner and barely say a word. I was so used to making him comfortable.

He used to sit on the side of the bed and sob at the thought of Henry. It if weren't for Henry he would have been gone long ago. I mean years and years ago. Not that he told me this, but I'd known it. For a long time I'd known it and worn it everywhere I went, like an ill-fitting pair of shoes.

Henry just happened to be standing in the living room talking to his friend Craig Merridan on the phone and staring out the window when he noticed his father's car gliding slowly down their road.

"Oh my God," he said in the middle of one of Craig's long-winded descriptions of some science fiction movie he'd seen on TV.

"What?" Craig said.

"Oh my God." Henry stepped closer to the window and looked out.

"What?" Craig shouted.

"My father just drove by."

"He did? You mean he just drove by, or did he drive by slowly or something?"

"Slowly, like he was spying on us."

"Wow," Craig said, obviously not quite knowing how to respond.

"Listen, I got to go, I'll call you later." Henry hung up and went out onto the front porch and listened for a minute. Because the road was a dead end he knew his father would have to drive back before long. When he heard the car coming he stepped down onto the lawn and stood behind one of the trees. His heart was beating wildly, and when the headlights appeared slowly around the curve Henry stepped out into the road. The car stopped and Henry walked around to the driver's side. His father, sitting with a foolish expression on his face as if he'd been caught stealing, didn't look at Henry. He just stared straight ahead through the windshield.

Henry was breathing so hard he could barely talk. "What the hell are you doing, Dad?" he said.

His father shrugged and shook his head very slowly.

Henry felt furious suddenly, and he leaned down and put his face close to his father's. "What are you looking for, Dad? Huh?" His teeth were clenched and he was talking in a voice he didn't think he'd ever heard himself use. "What do you think you're going to see?" He now started to shout. "If you had any guts at all you would go in and look at Mom, you'd go in and see what your screwing around has done to her instead of driving by like some crazy spy. Well, go to hell!" He took his finger and poked hard into his father's collarbone. His father, still not having looked once at Henry, took his foot off the brake and stepped on the accelerator. The car jerked forward and zoomed off down the road and Henry stood there watching it go. His whole body had started to shake.

Only when the car disappeared over the hill did he turn and start back towards the house, noticing for the first time his brother standing out on the porch in his pajamas. Henry stopped there on the front lawn and stared at him.

"What was he doing?" Mathew said.

Henry shook his head, then looked down at his own bare feet in the overgrown grass of the lawn. He suddenly felt dizzy; everything was spinning around him. He could still feel the hardness of his father's collarbone under his finger, still hear his own words stabbing away in his head.

"Are you okay?" Mathew said.

Henry lifted his hands and looked at the backs of them; they were fluttering like butterfly wings. "I don't know what the hell he was doing. He was driving by, spying on us or something." But his anger had left him now and his voice felt flat and empty.

"Huh," Mathew said. "Well, he probably won't do it again." And he walked back inside. Henry stared down at his hands for another few seconds, then he followed his brother into the house.

Bette came over later that night. She was wearing her pair of brilliant pink bike shorts, both her arms covered with her silver bracelets, and within five minutes she was asking Henry what was wrong. He was stoned, sitting down at the kitchen table leaning over the newspaper's classified section, still looking for a car.

"How do you know there's anything the matter?" he said.

"I can tell, so what happened?" She plopped down onto his lap. She strung her two tans arms around his neck and pressed her face against his throat. He sat there for a minute like a block of stone; then he felt everything soften and he put his arms around her.

Only a few weeks in his life and he couldn't imagine what it had been like before her. He would try sometimes, his mind would ache back, but life then seemed strangely blank.

"Did you see your dad, Henry?" she whispered.

He nodded but his throat was so tight he couldn't get any words out.

"Ah," she said, her lips up to his ears, "thought so."

Mathew got a cold just lying alone up in his room. This proved his point even more. There had to be something wrong with him. He barely had contact with anyone and bang, he came down with a full-blown cold right in the middle of July. Somewhere in the back of his head he had the needling thought that he wasn't long for this world.

To top off the whole lousy situation he ran out of vitamin C and garlic tablets and herbal cough drops, and after two days of lying in bed drinking nothing but peppermint tea and water he decided it was time to pull himself together and get to the nearest health food store. He found one in Madly, the next town over, listed in the phone book. And he bundled himself up in an old wool scarf and sweater and made the drive through the eighty-degree heat.

He'd just stepped into Good For You Foods, unable to breathe through either nostril, sweat trickling down his back, when someone came up behind him and said, "Hey!" so loudly that his two feet lifted from the ground. When he spun around, Henry's girlfriend was standing there with her hands on her hips, grinning up at him. "Hey! I almost didn't recognize you without your pajamas on!" she said, laughing. The very person he spent most of his time hiding from up in his bedroom.

Words simply failed him at the sight of her. He felt his face go red, took a few steps backward, and bumped into a display of oat bran cereal. She reached out her hand. "Come on!" she said. "Don't you remember? Bette, Henry's girlfriend."

Mathew put out what he knew was a hot sweaty hand and they shook. He still hadn't said anything except for muttering one long "Uhhh," after which his mind had gone absolutely blank.

"Did Henry tell you I worked here? He told me you were into healthy stuff and I told him to tell you to come down. Did he?"

"Uh, well, actually," Mathew managed to get out, "no, no, he actually didn't."

She made a clicking sound with her mouth and rolled her eyes. "Geez, I told him to tell you but I knew he wouldn't. He's a space-out."

"Uhm," he said, "well, I guess I'd better finish shopping." He lifted the piece of paper he'd written his list on and saw his hand was shaking. He tucked it into his jacket pocket. "Actually that's about everything. I guess maybe I should pay."

She hadn't moved; she was still smiling at him. "You sure?" she said, and reached forward and gently pulled the list back out of his pocket. She brought it up close to her face and her eyebrows squeezed together as she examined it. "Wow, no offense or anything but you have worse chicken scratch than my sister and I didn't think that was possible. Are you a lefty?"

"Uhm, yeah." Mathew unconsciously tucked his left hand into his jacket.

"Thought so, most smart people are," she said, still scrunching up her face in an effort to read his list. "Let's see . . . you got millet and vitamin C and garlic tablets and what kind of shampoo did you get— greasy or dry?" She looked up at him.

"Huh?"

"Greasy or dry hair, which kind do you have?"

"I guess I don't know," he was mumbling.

"Let's see," she said, pressing her lips together and inching even closer to him. She came around to his side and stood up on her tip-toes. "Huh."

He stood still and glanced at her out of the corner of his eyes; she was studying his hair with a deeply contemplative expression.

"Dry," she said flatly. She took the shampoo out of the basket and looked at it and shook her head. "Thought so, guys always use the wrong kind of shampoo, they just get whatever they see first and it's always wrong. This stuff could clean the grease off your stove." She walked over to the cosmetics shelf and put the shampoo back and picked up a different bottle. She read the label. "Here, this is better," she said, and came over to him again, her sandals clapping across the brick floor. "Tell me how you like it."

"Thanks," Mathew said, and started towards the cash register. "Welp, I guess I should pay now."

"Wait a second." She was studying the list again. "Did you get rice?"

"No, I guess I didn't."

She walked across the store and he heard her say, "You ever had this Texmati stuff?"

"Uh, I don't . . . I don't think so."

She came back towards him waving a box. "Oh, it's really good, give it a shot." And she dumped it into his basket.

"Thanks," he said, trying once again to get over to the cash register.

"Hang on there." She was back at the list. "I'll get you some soy milk and then you're done."

She went off and came back with the soy milk, carrying it over to the cash register. " 'Kay," she said, and patted the counter for him to put his basket up. He placed it on the counter, then stepped back and looked down at the floor where he was standing. His heart was now doing triple time in his chest and he truly felt he needed to sit down. Bette laid everything out on the counter and rang up each item, saying the price out loud before she punched in the numbers. "That'll be twenty-three dollars and fifty-two cents but you can make it fifty."

Mathew jabbed his hand into his pocket and brought out his wallet. His hands were still shaking as he pulled out a twenty and a five and handed them to her.

"Thank you," she said in a crisp businesslike voice. She made change and handed it back to Mathew, counting out: "Fifty makes twenty-four and one makes twenty-five."

As Mathew was putting the dollar back in his wallet Bette started bagging his stuff. It surprised him that she wasn't asking any questions. It in fact occurred to him that maybe he had offended her by not talking to her. "Well, I really appreciate it," he managed to get out. "Thanks for the help."

She waved her hand. "Oh, don't mention it. I'm pretty bored in here so any activity is kind of welcome."

Mathew took his bag and met her eye for a brief second. She didn't seem to look offended. She was smiling, looking right back at him. "Well," he said, and took the bags. "So, I guess I'll see you later."

"All right." She crossed her arms over her chest and gave him a serious look, her eyebrows pushing together. This made him start to feel weak again. "Hey," she said. "I mean, sorry I startled you before. I mean just now, and on the stairs that night, too."

Just the mention of the night on the stairs made Mathew want to shrink out of sight. He shrugged. "Oh well . . ." And started backing away.

She came around from behind the counter and pulled open the door for him. "Take care of that cold," she said. "I know what a drag it is, I'm just now getting over mine."

Mathew thanked her again and took off up the street at such a good clip his own legs surprised him.

It took him until later in the day to realize it must have been Henry's girlfriend who'd given him the cold. And as much as this relieved him, knowing now that it wasn't just out of nowhere that he got sick, it also made him want to tuck himself away from her all the more, like a turtle pulling himself clean into his shell and coming out only when the coast was clear.

It seemed hardest in the middle of the day. The light trying to get past the closed shade, the tangled sounds of life going on outside, voices and cars and lawn-mowers. I felt like an opened wound there in my bed. The air itself stinging me. And there was nothing to say. Nothing to even think about. No notion of what day it was, if it was still sometime in July, or if July had in fact already slid into August. Not a longing left in me. Not a single urge. Not to eat or see anyone or be anywhere. Just my body laid out like a corpse. The only thing that didn't quit was my heart. It kept on and on, pumping through the day, pounding and banging straight into the night.

It had started to rain, so Jeff and Henry were forced to quit work early. Henry came home, took a shower, then lay down on his bed, and after listening to the light rain falling for a bit he fell asleep. He'd been staying up late every night with Bette and getting up at seven every morning. Not to mention all the pot he'd been smoking during the day with Jeff. He was exhausted, and now he slept as if he were catching up, deeply, his breath long and slow and steady.

He slept from two o'clock until five forty-five and probably would have kept on sleeping had it not been for a loud squeaking noise coming from downstairs that made him sit right up out of his slumber. He opened his eyes and listened, then got off his bed and went and stood at the top of the steps. The squeaking paused for a second, before it started up again, and a few seconds later Bette appeared around the corner dragging a large suitcase behind her. She looked up at him.

"What's going on?" he said.

"Can I stay here?" she whispered. "I can't be there anymore, my mother's going to drive me crazy. I mean, seriously."

"Bette." He started down the stairs. "What happened?"

She shook her head. "Is it okay if I stay here for a bit, Henry?"

A few minutes later he was lugging her suitcase up the stairs and she was following him. It hadn't occurred to him how little he really knew about her life. But he wasn't sure it mattered. He shut the door of his room and they fell onto the bed, her skin hot under her tee-shirt and her lips up against his ear. "Henry," she was whispering, "hold on to me, okay?"

Mathew saw her taking the suitcase out of the trunk of her car and he almost passed out with despair. He was up in his bedroom looking out the window and he saw her down in the driveway in a red dress, struggling to get the massive thing out of the trunk. He sat down on the side of his bed and put his head in his hands.

Later that day when he tiptoed into the bathroom and closed the door, he froze at what he saw. The room was crammed with her things, pink jars of cream and powder, half a dozen assorted bottles of shampoo around the edge of the bathtub, a fluorescent-pink bathrobe hanging over his mother's old blue one, a light blue box of tampons next to the toilet, and the dense smell of her perfume, clutchingly sweet, draping itself like a heavy cloak on the air.

Chapter 6

She was the first person in over a month who just walked right into my room. No knocking, no warning, nothing. She flung the door open, walked in, and said, "Hey Mrs. Iris, how are you?"

I sat up on my elbows and tried to focus: she was a burst of color and gum snapping and some kind of sweet perfume. "Bette," was all I could get out.

"So I'm getting Henry to bring up the TV," she said, and stepped out into the hall. I heard her call down the stairs, "What's taking you?" Then she stepped back in and smiled and shrugged and started walking around my room examining the photos and paintings and books. "Wow," she said, stopping at my bureau and leaning into the photograph of Gordie, the one of him taken at his first art opening in New York. "That's him?" She looked at me over her shoulder.

I gave her a nod.

"Wow." She picked up the photograph to inspect it closer. "I

thought he'd look different. I guess he's kinda nice-looking but . . ."
And she shrugged and looked over at me again.

I heard Henry slowly coming up the stairs one step at a time.

Bette walked out into the hallway and said, "Geez, that thing is
prehistoric. Wow, don't tell me it isn't color."

"Nope," I heard Henry grunt.

"No!" she screamed. "Classic! I mean black-and-white TVs are
practically antiques now."

She came back in the room. She was still holding the photo of
Gordie and she looked around. "Let's see, you want to be able to see
it from your bed, so maybe if we put the set on the bureau. I mean it'll
block the mirror but that's all right, isn't it?" She turned to me with
her eyebrows raised up and her gum going off like machine gun fire
from her mouth.

"I guess," I said.

Henry came through the door a second later looking over at me
nervously and apologetically. "Here, put it on there and we'll see how
it works," Bette said, directing him to the bureau. Henry had his
work boots on and his hands were black with grease. He put it down
on the bureau and the two of them stepped back and looked at the
monster of a thing. Bette turned to me. "What do you think?"

"Well, I really never watched much TV," I told her, gently, because I didn't want to hurt her feelings.

"That's what Henry said but I figure it's not too late to start. I mean
you don't have to, but it does give you something to do. I mean, watch
a couple of soap operas in the afternoons or something, they're made
just for this kind of thing."

Henry was standing there looking at me and he shrugged. She still had hold of the photo of Gordie. She sighed and walked over to the edge of my bed and sat down and said, tucking the gum somewhere in her mouth and making her voice gentler, "Just give it a try and if you can't take it, we'll move it. Okay?"

"Okay," I said.

"All right then, Henry, plug her in."

He plugged in the set and Bette got up and turned it on. Three stations came in and after flicking back and forth a few times she left on some game show. "That's Vanna White," Bette said, pointing to a thin blond woman who was turning over blocks of letters. "She looks better in black-and-white actually." Bette walked over and lifted up one of the blinds and looked outside. I could smell her banana-flavored gum and I was watching her with the photo of Gordie still in her hand. She glanced over at me and said, pointing to the shade, "Mind if I leave this up for now? It's so nice out it's a shame to have it down."

I said, "All right."

Then she walked back over to the bureau. "I'll just stick this in here, okay?" and she opened my top drawer and put the photograph of Gordie underneath my stockings and underwear and gently closed the drawer again. Bette looked at me and then at Henry and laughed. "Wow, don't look so freaked out! I mean, let's face it, he's the last person she needs staring at her right now."

We turned to the TV and Bette plopped down on the foot of the bed and started calling out letters to the blond woman with the small body and the big head.

Henry had stopped being able to remember what it was his mother had always done. He'd think, rummaging around in his memory, but he couldn't seem to find anything concrete. He knew she had cooked and cleaned the house and shopped and sometimes sat down in the study with the newspaper, but beyond all that he couldn't picture her. He couldn't imagine her talking or laughing or enjoying herself at all. It was frustrating; at first it made him feel as if he had a terrible memory.

Then one night, when he was sitting in the corner of her room and she was lying in bed, blinking and blinking, a sad thought slipped into his head. Something that had never occurred to him before. It was the notion that she had in fact always been like this, maybe cooking dinner, maybe vacuuming the living room but always just like this, sad and vacant and letting the days go by and by.

After that the darkness and stillness of her room felt as if it swallowed him whole, and he stopped going in to see her at all. Not that it helped him; he still got the same sunken feeling every time he reached the top of the stairs and saw her door, every time he pictured her. It was as if he were diseased by her, while he was with Bette two rooms away, while he was mowing lawns, while he was smoking pot with Jeff, eaten at not only by the thought that she'd come to a stop but by the other thought now too, that nothing much had changed.

Mathew got through almost the entire day before he realized it was his birthday. He would have completely forgotten had he not accidentally been turning past a radio station around nine that night when the announcer said, "Two days until August, then summer's half over. Bummer, man." He switched off the radio and lay there on his bed feeling stunned. He'd never been much for birthdays; in fact he usually managed to disappear to avoid all the commotion his mother was always trying to stir up, but he'd never actually forgotten it before. This sent a stampede of heartbeats through his chest. The whole thing made him feel a little as though he were disappearing.

Just a year ago he had worked straight through his birthday. He had woken up in his little apartment and headed for the library, where he sat all day slumped over his books, the world falling back away from him, his mind fully focused and working like a neatly oiled machine. He had come home to find a package by his door and he had taken it into his apartment, placed it on the couch, and after eating dinner and doing a little more reading opened it with not the least bit of enthusiasm. He knew it was from his mother and knew it probably wouldn't be anything he needed. And sure enough, after he had unwrapped the paper and opened the Happy Birthday card, he pulled an odd little salt and pepper shaker set out of the box. He made a face, holding the things in his hand. He went over and put them on his little card table where he ate his dinner, stepped back, looked at them, then put them in his cabinet, where they stayed and where he ended up leaving them when he packed his things.

Now, thinking about his mother sending him the unwanted wooden set made him roll over on his bed. He imagined her picking them out at some store, wrapping them, then going all the way to UPS to have it sent to him. The card had said something like, "Happy Birthday, honey. Hope you are well. We miss you. Love, Mom and Dad and Henry." She had signed for all three of them.

She had always driven him crazy on his birthday. When he was little she would make hats for him out of colored construction paper. She'd sit cross-legged on the floor like a kid, stapling and taping, while he sat on a hard upright chair reading one of his books. Even then she'd gotten on his nerves with all her fussing. She would cook a big birthday meal for him—he liked fish best even as a kid—and she'd make him wear the hat while he ate. There were pictures of him wearing those big Indian headdress hats she'd made, sitting in front of a glowing cake, the only bland thing in the picture being his face, his little mouth as flat as an ironing board, his hazel eyes staring dead into the candles, and his skin just as white as the frosting on the cake. Thinking of all this now made him feel unbearably sad and a big knot formed in his throat so it was hard for him to breathe. He'd cried so few times in his life that it was a strange feeling indeed, the way the tears came up suddenly in his eyes and rolled down warm and slow into his ears. He couldn't figure out if he was crying for himself whose birthday had been forgotten or for his mother who had made him all those unappreciated hats.

It surprised him, how many tears kept rolling down his face. He didn't make any noise really, the way some people did; he just blew his nose a few times and hiccuped a little when he inhaled deeply.

It was now ten o'clock and he could hear Henry and his girlfriend down in the living room listening to music and talking. (It amazed him that two people could find that much to talk about.)

He decided to sneak out and wash his face, which in the little mirror above his bureau looked red and swollen, so he quietly opened his bedroom door and tiptoed across the hall, but right before he was about to go into the bathroom he changed his mind and knocked very gently on his mother's door. There was no answer but he opened it anyway and stepped into the pitch-black room.

"Mom?" he whispered, shutting the door behind him and looking in the dark towards the bed.

There was a moment before she stirred, and again he said, "Mom?"

"Henry?" she said quietly.

"No, it's me, not Henry."

"Mathew?" she said.

His eyes had started to adjust and he could just make out her face, pale and turned towards him.

"Yes, Mom, it's Mathew. I came in here to tell you it's my birthday today."

She sat up in bed and rubbed at her face. "It's your birthday," she said, repeating it to herself.

"I just thought I should tell you," Mathew said, only now wondering why exactly he was telling her. "I just wanted to tell you," he said.

"Your birthday?" Her voice was small.

"I remembered about those hats you used to make me, Mom. I was thinking about them and I was wishing I had been a nicer kid."

"Oh, honey," she said softly.

He felt the knot in his throat starting up again and he looked down towards the floor. He was barefoot and the skin on his feet was so white that they seemed to glow in the dark.

"I just wanted to tell you I appreciated the hats and the salt and pepper thing too."

"The salt and pepper?"

"You sent me a set of salt and pepper shakers last year on my birthday and I probably didn't even thank you."

"Oh honey," she said again, her voice this time filled with sadness.

"But I thought I should tell you it was my birthday, Mom, I don't even know why. I just thought somehow I should tell you."

He saw her nod and he backed up towards the door and reached for the knob, but before he stepped out into the hall she said, "Happy birthday, Matty." And when he heard it he realized it was the reason he'd gone into her room, a little like throwing a life preserver out in the dark and after a moment feeling her reach for it after all.

The TV did nothing but show me a dark reflection of myself lying in bed. My two big feet and miles down from them, my puny head. When I was awake I stared at it and it became a kind of landscape of hills and plains.

The thing is I got so lost most of the time. I got lost and couldn't find what it was I was lying there for. Oh, I knew. I knew Gordie was gone, but I could handle his absence by then. Not to say it didn't pain me; there'd been no pain like that ever before. But I could sustain that. It was rather the fact that he wasn't dead that worked me like a pin on a balloon, stabbing me and leaving me airless. Flat out. It was the fact that he was still getting up in the mornings and brushing his teeth and eating his meals and speaking his words. That he was still on the earth and he was on it without me. And this thought caused me not so much pain as bafflement. It came into my head but slipped right back out like an old dollar bill in a change machine.

Sometimes I'd even hear myself say, "No," when I didn't even think I was thinking about it. But of course I did nothing but think about it.

Birds starting up before light. Wind rattling the leaves of the big maple. A car passing with its radio on. I did nothing, nothing, nothing but think about it.

Chapter 7

By August Henry noticed that the lawn had turned into field, high, wavering in the wind and ultimately making the house look as if it had sunk into the earth. A shutter on one of Mathew's windows had come loose in a storm weeks back and now tilted permanently to the right, the porch was covered with sticks and leaves, and the left rear tire of his mother's Honda, parked in the driveway, had been flat since the beginning of July. It occurred to Henry that it looked like a set from some dumb horror movie.

He could tell that when their neighbors drove by they tended to slow down and lean a little to try and get a better look. This made him feel irritable. He thought maybe he should make a recording of someone screaming and play it full blast out the window. That would really give everyone something to talk about.

He knew he could easily mow the lawn. Jeff had offered several times to lend him the riding mower (the grass was so high now their old push mower wouldn't work), but he couldn't help feeling stubborn

about it. It was something his father always did and now that he'd
left, Henry wasn't going to fill in after him that easily. He liked the
idea of his dad driving by the house again and seeing everything in
total disarray.

On the whole, he had a hard time sorting out exactly how he felt
about his father. Most of it was anger but then under the anger he
felt pangs of sadness, too. He'd think of his father in his car the night
he drove by the house, the way he sat slumped down, looking
through the windshield, and it would burden Henry's mind for hours
afterwards.

He'd started to have dreams at night that he was doing awful
things to his father. Terrible dreams that he would describe to Bette
in the morning. Bette was the one who pointed out to him how passive
his father was in all these dreams. How pitiable. Henry denied it.

But then he kept thinking. It was true in the dreams his father just
stood there with this blank face. Almost like he was dead already.
And it was true Henry felt overwhelmed with sadness for his father
after he did these things to him. But the minute he woke up, his anger would float back in and he couldn't admit to these other feelings.
Bette, of course, managed to discover them without his help.

She was always pointing out things about himself he'd never really
taken the time to see. And she'd say them in a way that made them
come out as compliments. For instance, instead of just telling him he
was a slob, like most people would, she'd say, "You're definitely
someone who likes to play it loose. You don't like organizing things
because it takes away the spontaneity of life for you, and you thrive
on that. That's why your bedroom looks like it does." The things she
said made him sound interesting to himself and he enjoyed hearing

them and thinking about them later. "I can tell you have one of those weird IQs," she'd say, "not one of the normal ones where you're great at math or anything but the other kind that tests the other side of your brain. I bet if they gave you one of those tests you'd be way above average."

He never considered himself brainy like his brother but it was true, he knew he wasn't dopey, and certainly not boring. He'd always considered his way of thinking kind of interesting. But Bette was one of the few people who'd ever actually seen it in him. She saw it and valued it and this made him think differently about himself. He even felt a little more optimistic about his future after she said these things.

Bette was the one, in fact, who told him he was definitely artistic.

"I can tell," she said once when they were lying in his bed in the dark. "I can tell you're an artist at heart. Just the way your mind works and the way you get all spaced out, that's your artistic talents lurking."

This was what got him thinking about putting things together. He'd always fantasized about it in the back of his head but it wasn't until Bette confirmed it that these fantasies seemed to blossom up. It all started when he was looking through one of his father's old art books that had been lying around in the study and he got caught by a photo of an Alexander Calder sculpture—it was a mobile, made of metal, with hundreds of little odd-shaped pieces that floated through the air—and it triggered something in him. Just looking at it made him feel he was being spoken to, in a language he could actually understand. It made his heart start banging, and from then on he began thinking about piling things and nailing them together and welding pieces of metal onto other pieces of metal. Or taking apart two old beat-up cars and putting them back together all topsy-turvy. He found he had an endless number of ideas, so many that he spent entire days pacing back and forth behind the lawn mower, building one monstrosity after another in his head.

"That's all I think about now," he told Bette one night when he got back from work. She was home from the health food store, sitting in the kitchen with a cigarette and leafing through a new copy of *People* magazine.

"What did I tell you," she said, almost sounding bored. "You're an artist at heart. Well, get to it, bud! Go on, get out there and start creating."

"Out where?"

"In that empty studio out there, you fool!" she said.

"But that's my father's."

"So? Did he ever tell you not to use the place?"

"Well, not exactly."

"So?" she said again, smiling and leaning towards him. "Go to it, Lenardo."

"I think you mean Leonardo."

"Whatever it is I mean, get hopping!"

He shook his head, but later that night he wandered out to the studio for the first time since his father had left. He opened the barn door and stood there for a minute, unable to step inside. It was the smell of the paint and turpentine that hit him unexpectedly, a smell that had always been accompanied by the sight of his father sitting on his little swivel stool in front of a canvas. "Henny Henny!" he'd say. "How's lousy old school?"

The place was musty and hot inside and Henry flicked on all the overhead lights and walked around the large room, examining it as if he'd never quite seen it before. All the things his father had collected—the birds' nests, various animal skulls, odd pieces of wood, black-and-white photographs of people he'd painted.

The next day after work he walked back out to the studio and a little while later began hammering one of his father's old palettes to the leg of the swivel stool, which he had turned upside down. Then he stood back and looked at it. He was breathing hard, figuring out what next.

Mathew had always been scared of people but now it was worse. Before, he'd been able to be around other people but keep himself removed. It was a kind of talent that had come naturally to him all his life. He could sit on a bus filled with screaming kids, spit-balls pinging into the back of his head, and his mind would be else-where, either engrossed in the book he was reading or thinking over some complicated math problem, the numbers doing a kind of shim-mying dance in his head. He could tell this frustrated other kids when he was younger; ignoring them was the best defense around. Once in fifth grade one of his classmates grabbed hold of his tee-shirt while he was walking down the hall and Mathew simply kept walk-ing, the tee-shirt splitting down the back like a curtain parting on a stage. "Oh geez," he'd heard the other kid saying. "Oops. Sorry, Iris, didn't mean to rip your shirt."

But everything was different now. His concentration had flown off and disappeared and he was left distracted, unable to focus. All his life he'd leaned into one book after another, as if they were worlds he could transport himself to, but now he couldn't get through two sentences without worrying about his mother, or feeling annoyed about some car radio playing too loudly as it passed by, or overhearing Henry's girlfriend talking on the phone down in the living room.

In fact, he found that the worst distraction of all was Bette Mack. Even when she wasn't around, when her voice wasn't piercing the quiet of the house, she somehow managed to be present. Everywhere he looked she seemed to have taken over and left her mark. The long blond hairs in the bathroom sink, the refrigerator filled with her food, the pink sandals left in the middle of the living room floor, a bottle of nail polish and a nail file left right out on the kitchen table. He found himself thinking about her all the time. Envisioning her, hearing her rattling chatter in the back of his head.

Twice a day he'd get up off his bed and go into his mother's room. He'd just stand there feeling helpless. "Mom?" he'd whisper.

"Yes?" she'd say, not turning to look at him.

"Are you all right?" He could never think of anything else to say, though it was painfully obvious she wasn't in the least bit all right.

And the silence that followed the question seemed to fill his head the way a deafening noise would, not letting him sleep or read or even think straight.

"**I mean** you realize I'm like living here, right?" Bette said to me one night.

"I thought you might be," I told her.

"Well yeah, I mean, I didn't mean to be disrespectful or anything by not asking you, but I sort of figured you had enough on your mind."

I nodded.

"I mean the fact is I'm eighteen, so it's not like I've run away from home illegally or anything anyway." She sighed and leaned back in the chair and cracked her gum. "Although the way my mother's acting you might think I'd been kidnapped or something. But, well . . ." She shrugged and sighed. "What's new."

She'd been coming into my room every night, swinging open the door and bursting through with a tray of food. Things like Jell-O and clear broth and toast and light tea. Hospital food. She'd set it down on my night table then walk around the room and snap on all the lights, lift the shade, open the window wide, then remake my bed with me in it.

She had a way of ignoring me while still being there with me. Compared to Mathew and Henry, who would come in looking terrified and ill at ease, she'd float right in, keep herself busy, chat, turn on the TV, and the whole time manage to prod me to eat. And I'd eat. Not because I wanted to eat or because I liked what she fed me but because I'd come to learn she had a stronger will than I did, and until I finished everything on that tray she wouldn't set one foot out of the room.

"I mean she was driving me nutso," she said, and it took me a few seconds to pick up the threads of the conversation about her mother.

"I think 'cause she's without a boyfriend. I mean every time she doesn't have a boyfriend she starts cooking a lot and bossing us around, my little sister Anna—I told you about her, right? . . . You know, only an hour of TV a night, and time for a game of Scrabble. I feel sorry for my sister, I think I kind of abandoned her by moving out. She'll probably just get fatter being there alone with my mom. She's sort of fat now, I mean not real fat but chubby.

"Anyway"—she let a long sigh go and a second later her banana gum breath reached me—"I guess I've kind of had it. I mean she's been dragging us around ever since I was a kid and I told myself that this is the last stop for a while. For me anyway, even if it's not for her. How 'bout the rest of that toast, Mrs. Iris?"

She stood up and walked over to the window. She was barefoot and as silent as a cat. "I like it here anyway," she said. "I guess just the fact that this place isn't a rental. I mean I realized the other day I've never lived in anything but a rental and it's not really the same, is it?" She turned and glanced at me over her shoulder, noticing the food still left on my tray. "You'll be sick if you don't eat, Mrs. Iris. You got to eat." Then she turned and looked back out the window. She said, "Men aren't worth starving over. My mother could tell you that."

A little later, after she went out and shut the door, the quiet plowed up against me again. The high *pitch-pitch* of the peepers and the steady distant clap of Henry's hammer (Bette had informed me he was in the studio "making something"), coming down and down and down through the dark.

He pretty much used whatever he could get his hands on. Old junk that was sitting around the studio and the garage. Then things from the woods. Big odd-shaped dead branches and vines and pieces of rusted barbed wire.

At first Henry took the thing apart as much he put it together. He was working towards something, even though he had absolutely no notion of what that was. He just seemed to sense, not necessarily in his mind but more in his bones, when something was or wasn't right.

Almost every night he'd lose track of time. He'd tell himself he was only going to go out there and fiddle, but then he'd be up on the step-ladder trying to Krazy Glue an empty wine bottle to a piece of wood and he'd suddenly realize it was dark out, that he hadn't eaten dinner or seen Bette since early that morning.

Bette never came out to the studio. She told him she didn't want to see the sculpture until it was finished. "Otherwise it might screw up your creative, you know, momentum."

"Creative momentum?" he said.

She shrugged. "Don't worry, I'm plenty busy here."

Once when he came in from the studio late at night, he'd found her down in the library, sitting at his father's desk looking through the family photo album. "Who's this?" she'd asked him when he walked in.

"Dad," Henry said, leaning into the tiny black-and-white photo of his father, heavily bearded, wearing his old beret, standing next to a jeep.

"Hippy?" she asked in a flat matter-of-fact voice.

"Hippy?" Henry said. "Hmm, well yeah, I guess he was a hippy. I actually never thought of him that way."

"Uh-huh," she said, and flipped a few pages ahead. "And who's this, you or Mathew?"

Henry blinked at the photo of his mother holding an infant. She looked pretty, wearing her hair up in a ponytail. It suddenly shocked him how young she was. "Geez, I don't know, I think it's Mathew."

"That was my guess," Bette said. "The mouth."

"The mouth?" Henry looked at the baby's mouth in the photo.

"Sour," she said, and shut the book and turned and put her arms around him. As they kissed he felt her start chewing her gum slowly in the back of her mouth. He slipped his hands up under her shirt and moved them across her glassy skin. He closed his eyes but it seemed he was always distracted now. Even when he was with Bette it was as if he were being pulled away from her by what went on in his head. Thinking of his father in his car that night. Of his mother lying up in her bed. Even the thought of his odd reclusive brother started to make him feel unable to be happy.

Chapter 8

Finally there was no way around it. Mathew had to do his laundry. He'd run out of socks and underwear several days earlier and he'd been forced to recycle ever since. Plus, his sheets had taken on a damp musty smell that wasn't helping him sleep. And there was his towel. He'd started to get the feeling Henry's girlfriend had been using it. Not only did he keep finding it in different places in the bathroom but when he smelled it he was sure he could detect a hint of her perfume mingled in with the smell of the mildew.

So that morning, once the coast was clear, he shuffled out of his room with two stuffed pillowcases and made his way slowly down to the basement. He'd started to notice how weak he'd become from lying around. Not only had his muscle tone practically disappeared but just climbing the stairs seemed a major exertion. When he arrived in the basement he was clearly out of breath and a thin film of sweat had lifted out of his pasty white skin. He stepped forward and opened the lid of the washing machine, and the smell that rose up from within almost bowled him over. He staggered backwards. It was horrendous. Like something had died inside. He quickly clamped a hand over his mouth and peered in. It was chock-full of clothing and the clothing was covered with a light green, almost fluorescent mold. After a moment of horror and uncertainty about what to do, he looked around, found the detergent, dumped two heaping cups inside, closed the lid, made sure it was on a hot water cycle, and turned the thing on. Then he fled up the stairs into the kitchen.

He made himself a bowl of millet and sat down at the table and ate and waited until he heard the washing machine shut off downstairs. Then he slipped on a pair of dishwashing gloves, went back down, and slowly opened the lid and looked inside. The smell wasn't completely gone but it was better. Obviously in need of a good drying out. He reached in and started drawing out the contents with his gloved hand and only then did he notice it was his mother's clothing. Skirts and underwear and cotton shirts and a pair of gardening shorts. He realized it must have been practically the last thing she'd done before she quit.

It hadn't registered until then that the least he could do for her was to keep the house from falling apart. Until he saw that moldy laundry the thought simply hadn't occurred to him.

That morning, after putting her clothing in the dryer and starting a load of his own, he went upstairs and took every towel out of the bathroom and discovered while he was doing it that the wicker hamper behind the door was overflowing. Half of it was Henry's clothing, half his mother's nightgowns. He took it all downstairs and the day was dedicated to doing laundry. (He found a mountainous pile in Henry's room.) Carrying hot loads upstairs and folding and separating them in the living room, then going back down for the next. He did nine loads altogether. And by the time he was finished, after he had carried all the folded laundry to its various destinations, placing a pile on Henry's unmade bed (and taking note that his sheets needed to be done), hanging fresh towels in the bathroom, bringing a stack into his mother's room and leaving it quietly on the chair near her dresser—after all this he walked into his room and lay down on his freshly made bed and slept well for the first time in months, slept from six in the evening straight through until nine the next morning, waking up with his Chinese slippers, which he'd been too tired to slip out of, still cupping his narrow white feet.

It took me a while to realize she'd been leaving things in my room. First it was a small needlepoint pillow that I had made years and years ago. She left that on the chair in the corner and it didn't occur to me that she'd left it until halfway through the next day, after I'd stared at it all that morning. Next she left a small photograph of my mother. It was a photo that had been hanging down in the hallway among all the other family photos as long as I can remember. She brought this up and left it on my nightstand and when I woke up the next morning the first thing I saw was my mother's small dark eyes looking over at me. Next she left an old Indian basket that I must say I have a certain attachment to, something I found in a junk shop a few years ago that I kept stray buttons in. She left this on Gordie's night table on the other side of the bed and again I found myself, when I was lying on my left side, studying its intricacy, imagining the woman who made it, her hands going like little animals.

She started leaving newspapers on the floor beside my bed, each one opened and folded to some new horror story. Car accidents, lost children, murders. She'd take them away when she came back the next night but a few days later another would appear. "Child Drowns in Bathtub." "Mother of Five Fatally Struck by Lightning." And she was right, they seemed to be the first company I'd had since Gordie left. Those horrible stories, just caked with other people's pains.

When I first saw the cigarettes on the windowsill I was sure they were hers and that she'd left them by accident. An unopened pack of Ultra Light Merits and a purple Bic lighter. But after staring for days at the Surgeon General's warning I finally came to the conclusion that they were mine.

The first one I smoked was at three o'clock one morning after the house had gone solidly quiet. It was the first cigarette I'd ever smoked. Half my body leaning out the open window into the cool night air, my blue nightgown billowing a bit in the wind, and my hand fanning the smoke away like a lone wing. And me thinking as I winced at the taste of the thing about the nun who sat down beside me on the bus to Evanston. Two days before I met Gordie. She was like a big open highway sign that said to me in large clear letters, "Go this way!" But for whatever reason I went right on past and—no wonder—here's where I wound up.

Henry dreamed he walked into the studio and his father was there working on his sculpture. In the dream he felt confused. At first he thought it was his father's sculpture but then halfway through he realized it was his own and his father was screwing it up. "Hey!" he said and his dad smiled at him and said, "Hey Henny!" in a sing-songy kind of voice before he turned and went back to work on Henry's sculpture.

Henry woke up after that and just lay in bed. It was six-fifteen and he had another forty-five minutes before he had to get up and get ready for work. Bette was curled on her side away from him. She slept in silence. It was light out and the sound of birds was thick and tangled up in the air. He lay on his back with his hands cupped behind his head and looked through a crack in the shade. He could see the sun coming in through the trees.

The day before, he'd gone to the Salvation Army after work (Bette's idea, she lent him her car) and not only did he find an old mannequin but he'd found an entire carload of stuff, including an old school desk, a plastic lobster, a prehistoric-looking waffle iron (the only piece he didn't intend adding to his sculpture), and best of all a huge pair of white golfing shoes that looked like they'd been caught in a flood. Altogether he'd only spent $13.43.

He'd worked until midnight. Taking the mannequin apart was easy but getting the school desk attached at an angle near the top of the sculpture was more difficult. He had to stand on top of his stepladder and try to hold the thing with one hand while he wound heavy wire around the legs. After he finally got it to hold pretty steady he realized the body of the mannequin, which he wanted to put into the chair of the desk, didn't sit on its own, especially at such a severe angle, so he had to tie the headless body into the chair. This gave it more of a violent look than he'd intended. It made it look like a sick crime when he originally just wanted it to symbolize the way he'd felt at school, as if his body might be there but the rest of him was always someplace else. But in the end he left it the way it was.

After thinking about his sculpture for a bit he sat up in bed and swung his legs over to the side.

"What time is it?" Bette said without moving.

"Early," Henry said. "Go back to sleep."

"Where are you going?"

"Studio," he whispered. "Go back to sleep."

He slipped into his shorts, the ones he'd slipped out of last night, grabbed his work boots, and tiptoed out of the room. He went downstairs and sat in the kitchen and put on his boots; then he walked out through the wet grass to the studio. In the dream his father had been humming while he worked—Henry remembered this as he pulled the door open and stepped into the room.

The sun was coming through the windows in long boxes of light and one of these caught and shone on a patent leather golfing shoe. "Hello there," he said out loud, striding into the room and pressing the play button of his ghetto blaster. Bob Dylan sang while Henry rubbed his hands together and tried to decide whether the lobster should dangle alone or be held in one of the mannequin's forlorn hands.

Mathew made a schedule for himself that he wrote out and pinned to his old bulletin board. Mondays he'd vacuum. Tuesdays and Thursdays were laundry days. Wednesdays he'd clean the kitchen and bathrooms. And Fridays he'd shop. He now had to travel three towns away to go to a health food store where he wouldn't run into Henry's girlfriend.

In the mornings he'd lie in bed until he heard her car roar out of the driveway. He'd wait for the small yelp of her tires as she turned onto the main road before he ventured from his room.

On this particular morning he'd woken at seven and had to wait until eight-fifteen before she left. He'd spent most of the time pacing around the room chewing on his fingernails, making plans for the day. It was Tuesday and he had a big load of laundry that needed to be done. He planned on stripping everyone's bed, his own and Henry's and his mother's if he could convince her to get out of it for a few minutes while he changed the sheets.

When he heard the girlfriend's car screech off down the road, he opened his door and stepped out into the hallway. The house was as deeply quiet as it always was, and he stood for a minute listening to its silence before he went downstairs and made himself a quick breakfast of brewer's yeast and oat bran mixed with a small amount of soy milk. Not the best thing he'd ever tasted, but he was so hungry he tried not to think about it.

He then put on the big apron that said "MOM" on it—he wore this to protect his old tee-shirt and boxer shorts from getting covered with lint—and went back upstairs carrying the laundry basket in front of him.

He knocked on his mother's door. She didn't answer, so he knocked again a little louder and said, "Mom, can I come in?" After hearing nothing in return he finally gathered the courage to crack open her door and stick his head into the stale air of the room.

"Mom," he said softly, "I'm doing laundry. Would you mind letting me get the sheets off your bed. I'll put some clean ones on at the same time."

She had her back to him and he didn't know if she was awake until she said, "It's okay, these are all right." She didn't even turn to face him.

Mathew just stood there. He'd had his heart set on putting clean sheets on her bed. He waited for the longest time, staring at her back, the laundry basket dangling from one hand beside him. He was wondering if he should ask her again but he finally just backed out of the room and shut the door quietly.

He turned and walked slowly over to Henry's door and pushed it open. When he saw the contents of the room he let out a small groan. It was a disaster area and it reeked of B.O. There were piles of clothing everywhere, stretched-out tee-shirts and greasy shorts and underwear flung this way and that. He leaned down and started picking up things with the tips of his fingers and dropping them into his basket.

He'd worked halfway into the mess when he lifted one of Henry's nasty socks and found underneath it a pair of pink underwear covered with red hearts. He stopped short and stared at them while an entire flood of heartbeats took over his chest. They were tiny and rolled up as if they'd been removed hastily. They had caught him off guard and he felt unable to make any kind of move. Should he pick them up and wash them? No. Then she would know that he washed her underwear and this thought made him feel extremely uneasy. Should he just leave them where they were? Alone, twisted, staring at him in the middle of the room? This didn't seem like a good idea either, seeing that then she would know he saw them and chose to just leave them there, like some kind of message.

Finally, after staring bent over at the pair of underwear, he came up with a solution. He would simply kick them under the bed; that way she would think he hadn't even seen them. Using his Chinese slipper, he carefully guided the pink panties underneath Henry's sagging unmade mattress. It wasn't until he let go a large breath of relief that what he'd thought was a mound of sheets on Henry's bed suddenly sat up and said, "Wow! What time is it?"

This came as such a shock that he somehow managed to cross Henry's room and get back over to the door without either of his feet touching the ground. He grabbed hold of the doorframe and tried to stop himself from passing out.

"Oh my *God!* It's you!" she practically screamed. "Holy mackerel, you scared the crap out of me! Wow! Whew!"

Mathew clung to the wood and tried to breathe deeper, but his head was in an utter fog.

"Jesus! I swear," Henry's girlfriend was saying. She was now sitting on the side of the bed with a sheet wrapped around her, its whiteness matching the pallor of her face. "Jesus, when you jumped like that I swear I almost had heart failure. I swear I thought you were an animal. You looked like an animal the way you moved."

Mathew was beyond words. He still hadn't gained control of his wobbly legs. I'm about to die, was the thought going through his head. I'm going to die. This is how someone like me dies.

"Hey, are you okay?" he heard her saying, and her voice reminded him of one of those drills at the dentist's office. The last thing he saw before he sank to the floor was the girlfriend moving towards him with the sheet wrapped around her body, and right before his head dimmed out and fell backward he had the strange thought that maybe she was actually an angel coming to take him up.

I finished that whole pack of cigarettes. It took me about five days. And by the fifth day I was a smoker. At night I'd get up and open the window and stand there and smoke and smoke and watch those big white lungfuls float off one after the other like clouds or ghosts going out into the darkness.

Jeff had to stop off at the drugstore over in Madly to get a few things and Henry wandered in behind him, stoned, wearing his cutoffs and work boots and his Bob Dylan tee-shirt. He knew he could have walked a few blocks down to the health food store where Bette was working, but for some reason he didn't feel up to it. He'd started to feel quieter lately, more in his head, less like talking.

The place was heavily air-conditioned, smelling of candy and perfume. Jeff headed off in search of shaving cream and Henry wandered down the first aisle, aimless and slow, his hands in his pockets. The whole place struck him as harsh. The fluorescent lighting, everything packed in plastic, the crappy music playing. He was standing in front of the stationery section, looking down at different pads of paper, when he heard someone say, "Are you Henry Iris by any chance?" He turned and saw the minister or the priest—he wasn't sure what he was called—from the town's church. The man was holding a shopping basket, looking at him through a pair of thick glasses that enlarged his eyes.

"Uh." Henry had the feeling he was being arrested even though he wasn't sure what he'd done. "I guess," he heard himself say.

The man smiled. He was overweight and red-faced and even in the frigid store Henry could see the shine of perspiration lifting off his skin.

"Ah, I wasn't sure." The man's basket was filled with toilet paper and mouthwash and he shifted it from his left hand to his right. "I'm Reverend Desell. I'm not sure we've ever met."

Henry shrugged. "Maybe, I don't know." He felt trapped suddenly. He knew he probably reeked of dope and B.O. and he tried to take a step backward.

"Well, I've been meaning to make a trip up to your house. I've heard things aren't going too well for your family."

"Oh," Henry said. "Things are all right, actually."

"I see." The reverend paused. "Well, I just wanted to let you know that if you or your mother or your brother, if any of you need anything, I hope you'll let me know. I'd be happy to speak with your mother. Do you think she'd like a visit?"

"A visit. Uh, well, she's actually away," Henry said. "She's out in the, uh, she's in Illinois with my grandmother." He was hoping the reverend didn't know his grandmother had died two years ago. Jeff had come down the aisle now and was standing there listening to him.

"Oh, well then, I see." The reverend looked concerned. "All right. I just thought I'd put the offer out there. Just in case."

"Well, thanks anyways," Henry said. He glanced over at Jeff, who seemed to be grimacing for him.

"All right then, nice to see you, Henry."

"Uh, oh yeah, nice to see you, too." The words came out of Henry's mouth halting and awkward.

He turned to Jeff. "You ready?"

"Ready," Jeff said. "Better go."

The reverend smiled at Jeff, then turned and went off down the aisle.

"Oh man," Henry said as they were walking out the doors into the hot street. "I can't take this."

Jeff was quiet. They got into the truck. Henry ran his hands through his hair. "Man," he said, "I can't deal with this shit anymore. My fucking father."

Jeff sat for a minute, his hands on his lap. He didn't say anything but Henry could feel him listening.

"I mean, I don't even know why I'm protecting her. Who knows, maybe I'm not protecting her at all."

Jeff nodded. "Maybe you should let him see her, you know. It might not be a bad idea, he's a pretty nice guy I think."

"I couldn't. She'd hate it. She'd freak out if that guy walked into her room and saw her in bed in her nightgown."

Jeff shrugged. He waited another minute; then he leaned forward and started the truck. "Well," he said as he backed out into the street.

Henry was silent for the rest of the afternoon. And he felt silent too. Like he didn't even want to hear his own voice. He kept imagining himself asleep. He had an image of himself curled up in a dark quiet place, sleeping so deeply that nothing affected him.

When Jeff dropped him off at home he didn't walk into the house, he went straight out back to the studio, relieved to shut the door and be alone. He lay down across the old couch and looked up at his sculpture. It seemed ridiculous now.

A little while later when he heard Bette's car pull into the driveway, he didn't get up and go into the house to see her as he did every night. He simply lay still, listening to her car door shut, and after a second he heard her go into the house. He had the feeling he'd just quit something, even though he wasn't positive what it was. He felt he'd suddenly stepped out of the big dance that everyone else was doing, stepped out and sat down.

She'd obviously taken Mathew's fainting as a kind of green light. A kind of surrendering on his part. Because after that there was no stopping her. She'd knock on his door in the evenings before exploding into his room, practically blinding him in a rush of fluorescent colors and revealing halter tops. "Hey!" was how she'd begin. He'd sit up awkwardly on his bed and try not to look at her and do his best to hang on to the snaking conversation.

One night she propped a foot up on the desk and proceeded to paint her toenails red.

"This stuff can give you a bit of a buzz," she said. "So enjoy it while it lasts."

He swore it did, too, the fumes of the nail polish making his head swim so that he ended up pulling his shirt up around his nose. Suddenly, from outside, Henry's hammer started banging. She lifted her head and listened for a second, then went back to carefully painting one of her toes.

"Was that what your dad was like?"

"My dad?" Mathew spoke from underneath his shirt.

"Yeah, was he like that?"

"Like what?"

"Always out there." She pointed over her shoulder. "You know, wrapped up in his work."

Mathew thought for a second. "Uhm, well, I guess so."

"Uh-huh." She didn't look up from her completed foot, just sat back in the chair and put her other one onto the desk. "I thought so."

A few seconds later she said, "You're like a genius, right?"

"Oh, uh . . ."

"I can tell, you've got the pallor."

"The pallor?"

"Well, you know, no offense or anything but it's like all those kids in the honor society at school, same thing, same kind of, well, same look."

"Oh . . ." He was thinking.

A few seconds later, on her last toe, she said, "Anyway, I got to say, I don't like him that much, I mean from what I can figure out about him."

"Who?" Mathew looked at her. He didn't know what she was talking about.

"Gordie." She said his name as if he were an old friend of hers, and it took Mathew a moment to realize she was talking about his father.

My room was a clutter. She'd brought so much stuff upstairs by that point that there was no more space anywhere. Cookbooks were piled up on the bureau, Gordie's old shoes that he always kept downstairs lined the floor, a bird's nest I found years ago on Cape Cod on top of the TV, Mathew's ancient wool mittens, my gardening gloves and trowel. I had to pick my way across the room to the windowsill where my cigarettes were.

Then one night she came in and left a small photograph of Henry under my pack of cigarettes. I found it later in the night when I got up to smoke. When I snapped my lighter on I saw it there, lying on the windowsill, smiling up at me. A color photograph taken probably a year ago, Henry standing out on the lawn in the sun, squinting towards the camera. His hair was already long then but that kid in the photo had practically vanished now. I flipped it over and looked on the back and I was surprised to see Gordie's tiny neat handwriting. In pencil, in one corner, he'd written, "Henry, seventeen."

The next night when Bette came in I said, "How is Henry?"

She shrugged. "Welp, it's hard to tell. He's keeping to himself."

"I haven't seen him in so long."

"Oh well." Bette sat down on the side of my bed; she cracked her gum. "You're actually not the only one, Mrs. I. I mean he's not feeling all that social. I think he's kind of sparring with himself. You know?"

Later, after she left, I pulled the photograph out from under my pillow and placed it against the lamp next to the bed.

In the hospital the morning after I'd given birth, he was brought into my room and I nursed him for the first time and he took hold of my breast with his little rose of a mouth and sucked with such strength that it made me laugh out loud, and I had the funny feeling it was he who was holding on to me, pulling me back into the world, rescuing me from my quiet life with Gordie and Mathew. A life I hadn't realized, until I had Henry in my arms, that I needed rescuing from.

Chapter 9

That morning Jeff opened the studio door and started shouting, "Jesus, Henry! It's eight o'clock. I've been knocking on the front door of your house for half an hour, what the fuck are you doing? Get up, we got to get going."

Henry had fallen asleep on the studio couch. The night before, he'd gotten drunk on a bottle of red wine that he'd found in his father's liquor cabinet. When he cracked an eye open he saw Jeff with his hands on his hips, looking at his sculpture. "What in the hell is this?"

He sat up and groaned and rubbed his face. His head hurt like crazy.

"Did you make this thing?"

Henry nodded.

"Jesus." Jeff walked slowly around it. "Christ, Iris, you're one wacky dude."

"Thanks," Henry said. He had his eyes shut and he was sitting on the edge of the couch.

He heard Jeff walk over to him and stop. He opened one eye and grimaced up at him. Jeff had his hands on his hips again and seemed to be looking down hard at him.

"What?" Henry said.

"What's going on with you? What are you doing out here, anyway?"

Henry shrugged.

"What about your girlfriend?"

He'd closed his eyes tight again; his expression was pained. "She's still there. She's in the house."

"And? So why are you sleeping out here? Did you have a fight or something?"

"No. No fight."

"So why are you out here, and not in there?"

Henry shrugged and shook his head. He opened his eyes and looked over at his sculpture. It went probably twenty feet into the air now, crowned at the top with the headless mannequin bound to the desk with wire. "I've been making this thing." He motioned towards it.

Jeff was quiet for a minute, then he sighed. "You look like shit," he said. "I mean really, Iris. I don't know what you think this all is going to lead to, but you can pretty much bet it's not going to be good."

Henry didn't say anything; he sat still. He wasn't mad at Jeff but he wished he'd leave. More than anything now, he just wanted quiet.

"Well . . ." After a second Jeff let out a big breath. "Let's go, we're late as it is."

Henry didn't move. He thought for a while before taking his hands away from his head and looking up at him. "Listen, Jeff," he said in a low voice. "Listen, I got to quit."

Jeff's face dropped, then he threw his hands into the air. "What? Oh shit, don't do this to me, Henry, you're really going to screw me over if you quit, I'm already backed up!" He slapped his legs with his hands and circled the floor.

Henry sighed. "I feel too crappy. I mean, you know, all over, crappy."

"Shit!" Jeff socked a fist into his palm, walked over to the window and looked out towards the house. "Christ!" Henry heard him say under his breath. His hands were back on his hips. After a while he sighed again and walked back over to Henry. "All right goddammit," he said, but he didn't sound mad anymore.

Henry shook his head. "I'm real sorry."

"Yeah, yeah," Jeff said. "Why don't you take a few days and see how you're feeling. I can cover things for a week. But then I got to find someone else."

Henry nodded. "Okay."

Jeff started out of the studio but he stopped first in front of Henry's sculpture.

Henry looked at him looking at it.

"Well." Jeff shrugged. "I have to admit, Iris, you're a fucking piece of work. I mean, really."

After he left, Henry sat there on the side of the couch for a long time. He felt blank. Like things had stopped mattering. It wasn't a good feeling but it wasn't a bad one either. After a while he stood up and staggered out into the woods. He leaned against a tree for a minute before he knelt down and threw up.

In the evenings, now that it was no longer any use hiding up in his bedroom, Mathew would eat dinner with her down in the kitchen. She did the cooking, first bringing a tray of food up to his mother, then coming back and eating with him at the kitchen table. He had to admit she wasn't a bad cook. To his surprise, in fact, she was a vegetarian like he was and made simple decent-tasting food. Better than his bowls of millet and brown rice and steamed kale.

He was quiet around her still but that was mostly because she talked so much it was hard to say anything. But he was a little more used to her now. He'd sit and eat and listen and sometimes, though he wasn't sure, he'd sort of enjoy himself. He didn't look at her too much. Not only did he find her eyes too blue and direct (they still made him feel nervous) but a few times he'd glance over at her while she was standing at the stove, and the look of her lean tan legs and smooth arms brought on a whole new feeling that scared the hell out of him. It was a kind of slow burning that went down through his torso. It made him clear his throat and stand up promptly for a glass of water.

After dinner he'd do the dishes and she'd talk right through them. He started to feel he knew a lot about her. Her family and the places she'd lived and the fact she once took special reading classes because she was dyslexic. He'd leave the kitchen immaculate before they went upstairs, washing the floor before shutting out the lights. She'd talk him right up the stairs too, only stopping when he'd back himself into his room and politely say, "Uhm, well, good night." He'd shut the door and sit on the bed, half relieved but at the same time a little disappointed by the sudden quiet and the stale air of his room. He'd listen to her go in the bathroom, shower, then eventually go to bed. Then he'd quietly go into the bathroom himself and the room would smell dense with her powder and creams and toothpaste and he'd find himself taking it all in for a minute before brushing his teeth.

It wasn't that he wasn't aware of Henry's absence. He thought about it quite a bit in fact. Especially in the mornings when he'd find his clean kitchen in disastrous shape. There'd be muddy footprints going across the floor, leading into the dining room right up to the liquor cabinet. There'd be bowls of food that he had neatly put away the night before sitting out on the counter, half eaten, the fork still stuck in them. There'd be cigarette butts in the sink. Waffles forgotten in the toaster.

He finally got up the courage one night to ask Bette where his brother was. She seemed surprised that he'd asked. "Oh, you mean you realize you have a brother?" She smiled. "I thought you all just chose to ignore these kinds of things. Anyway, he's out there in the studio building his thing. I guess it's a sculpture, kind of. I haven't seen it, I figure I'm going to wait until it's done. But anyway, that's what he's doing. I can't tell you much else, 'cause I haven't seen much of him. Keeping to himself, I guess. Either that or he's dumped me and hasn't gotten around to telling me yet." She shrugged and for a rare moment went silent. She turned and began cutting an onion on the counter.

He sat up in his chair. He suddenly wasn't quite sure what to say to her. "Uh, oh, I was wondering what he's been doing out there."

She shrugged again. "Now you know. I think he quit his job too. But I'm not sure."

"Oh," he said. "Well." But he didn't get much farther. He couldn't think of anything else to say. But something had started to frighten him a little. Not so much his brother's reclusiveness (he was accustomed to ignoring Henry) but more the fact that Bette was around him all the time now. And when she wasn't he found himself replaying her in his mind, her words and her smile and the sound of her sandals snapping across the floor.

She fell asleep on my bed one night. She came in late, around ten o'clock, and asked if I minded if she watched a little TV. There was some show on with a laugh track and I lay there looking up at the ceiling while she sat at the foot of the bed and watched. I listened to the one-liners and the laughter come and go in steady, even waves. Then Johnny Carson came on. I got up and smoked a cigarette at the window and when I was finished I turned around and she was curled up on Gordie's side of the bed. I looked at her. Something about her sleeping face made me know her life hadn't been easy. It wasn't the first time I'd thought this but now I knew for sure. Her sleep looked too needed. Like she'd never gotten enough. Like she was clutching it to her.

When I got in bed I listened to her quiet breathing, almost silent there beside me, and I was reminded of my first year in the house with Gordie. The year we drove here from the Midwest and bought the place and moved in. The year I began to realize he might have married me but didn't want a lot to do with me. He worked in the studio, came in for meals, but he didn't want to know about me. He didn't ask, didn't quite listen if I told him, and what I remember most about that time before I had Mathew is the great relief I'd feel when I was asleep. When I was out cold, dead to the world, just dreaming.

The next morning when Bette woke she said, "Mrs. I.?"

I looked over at her; she was on her back staring up at the ceiling.

"Is he really all that great?"

"Who?"

"Gordie," she said.

I didn't say anything for ages. Not because I didn't have an answer but because my throat had gone tight as a fist.

Eventually she said, "I didn't think so."

I heard her start chewing a little while later and it dawned on me that she'd slept the whole night with a lump of gum stored somewhere inside that mouth of hers.

He'd walked into the house for a minute to grab a bottle of vodka from his father's cabinet (now close to being cleaned out), when he heard her say, "Henry." He turned. Bette was standing in her pink nightgown in the doorway. She looked a little shaken, like a kid awake from a bad dream. It was past midnight.

"What?" he said, and the word came out harder than he'd expected.

"I haven't seen you in so long," she said. "I mean, are we even still . . . like . . . together?"

His mouth clamped down tight suddenly and he just stood there, and stared at her, until finally she turned and walked into the dark living room and disappeared around the stairs.

He knew he'd just told her he didn't want her anymore. But he had no notion at all why he would do such a thing. It was some kind of torture, he knew that much. He felt it starting there, a dim pain that he sensed would do nothing but become unbearable. As he was walking back out to the studio through the grass, he stopped and took a long slow drink from the bottle. It went down smooth. Only after he stopped swallowing and started to walk again, only then did the back of his throat begin to burn.

When she opened his door late that night, Mathew sat straight up in bed and stared at her. She closed the door and the dark came down around her and he heard her say, "It's just me." But he didn't move or speak, he just sat there stone still in the dark while she pulled her dress up over her head and slipped out of her underwear. Even after she slid under the sheets he sat there, not moving, hardly breathing. She reached out and touched his back and he flinched, but she kept her hand there, her palm flat out on his hot skin until he felt his fear lift out of his body the way a big bird lifts out of a tree, slowly gathering its weight in its wings and flying off.

I dreamed about Bette, dreamed she was playing an instrument. A kind of accordion. She was down in the library and the music was pouring through the house. It was sort of sad music, yet at the same time it was comical. In the dream I got up out of bed and went down the stairs. And there she was on the couch, playing with her eyes closed, half smiling, half sad-faced, and naked as a jay bird except for a pair of large white shoes on her feet, the kind nurses wear, neatly laced and roomy.

Henry was draped over the couch in the studio drunker than he'd ever been in his life. Earlier, he'd fallen off the second rung of the little stepladder; he'd been wrapping a piece of chicken wire around a log and suddenly just tipped over and landed in a heap on the floor. He'd drunk almost the entire bottle of vodka. He was bombed. "I'm bombed," he kept saying to himself, "bombed-ola." Every time he tried to stand up he'd feel the floor flowing out underneath him, so he stayed there on the couch, staring up at his sculpture. The thing went from looking like a massive heap of junk to looking sort of magnificent, he thought, like a fabulous dinosaur bird.

He lifted the bottle and said, "I'm on the road to ruin!" and tried to take a swallow but missed his mouth by a long shot and wound up spilling vodka down his neck and shirt and onto the couch. "Road to ruin," he said again and this time he lifted the bottle higher and dumped it over his head and suddenly remembered the graduation party when everyone had cheered him on. "Henry! Henry!" He could see them all clearly, all his classmates standing around him yelling. "Henry," he said; then he shouted it, "Henry!" but it didn't come out as a cheer; it sounded more like he was calling to himself, standing out in the middle of a big field calling into the woods.

Chapter 10

On the day after the first night he slept with her he had a hard time believing it had happened at all. While he was vacuuming the kitchen floor he kept shaking his head. It was too bizarre. This was his brother's girlfriend. He shook his head again and sat down in one of the chairs, the vacuum cleaner still howling; he stared at the floor.

A minute later Henry walked into the kitchen from outside. He had two giant black rings looping under his eyes and his clothes looked as if they'd been worn for weeks. Mathew reached down and turned off the vacuum cleaner but Henry didn't even seem to notice him. He just opened the refrigerator door and stood there looking in.

"Henry?" Mathew said.

"Huh."

"How are you?"

"Swell," Henry said. He got two beers from the refrigerator and walked out of the kitchen. It was only eleven in the morning. Mathew watched through the window as he went across the lawn towards the studio. Halfway there he stopped and tilted his head and drank an entire beer; then he heaved the empty bottle into the woods behind the house.

Mathew's heart was thumping and he had a sickly feeling crawling through his stomach.

By the afternoon he decided the best thing to do was to just make like the whole thing had never happened. If he was lucky Bette would have come to the same conclusion and would never mention it to anyone and never talk about it again.

He didn't eat dinner with her that evening; he stayed in his room with the door shut. And by nine o'clock, when she still hadn't shown up, he started to feel safe. She'd obviously realized what a mistake they had made, and he turned off his light and closed his eyes.

Unfortunately, the dark only made things worse. She loomed right up in his mind. He couldn't stop thinking about her, that smooth skin, the warm breath, her body. He rolled over onto his side and looked towards the window. He told himself to stop.

But a little while later when his door opened and he heard her come into the room and slip out of her clothing, he couldn't help feeling he had willed her there.

It went on for a week. Her crossing the hall at night from Henry's room to Mathew's and then back in the early morning. I guess I could have put a stop to it. But I was far from that. I was beyond judgment.

Besides, it was like a cure for Mathew. He didn't shuffle during the days anymore; in fact he seemed almost spirited. Carrying stacks of clean laundry into my room, vacuuming the floor with a new fervor, and barely even noticing me.

She still brought me dinner every night. Maneuvering through the clutter, cracking her gum, snapping up the shades. She acted as if nothing unusual were going on. And I'm not even sure she saw it as that. It was more that she was going about her business. Doing what needed to be done.

By now Henry felt as if he had truly slipped away from himself. It was a strange feeling. He had spent a whole week in the studio, making only a handful of trips to the house to get supplies of food and beer and only one trip into town for a carton of cigarettes, two gallon jugs of red wine, and a box of doughnuts. He slept during the day on the old couch and stayed up through the night drinking and smoking the remainder of a bag of pot he'd bought from Jeff.

This is what he was up to that Saturday night. He'd just rolled himself a joint and was about to smoke it, when he discovered there were no matches anywhere. He went through every drawer in the studio, then walked over to the house and went through the kitchen, finally walking upstairs to his bedroom, where he kept a whole stack on his windowsill. The joint was dangling from his mouth as he walked into his room, grabbed a handful of matchbooks and stuck them into his pocket; then he walked out and went back down the stairs. At the bottom he stopped and lit the joint and it was during that pause in his movements, when he was holding still, that he heard Bette's voice, and only then did it occur to him she hadn't been in his room. He backed up a few steps and listened and sure enough he heard her again, talking in a low voice, a voice he recognized from his own late-night conversations with her—and every so often he'd hear Mathew respond.

He stood there for quite a while because he couldn't seem to move any of his muscles. Even though he was drunk the reality of what was going on up there in his brother's room started sinking right in and he found he didn't know what to do. He wasn't even sure how he felt. At first he thought it might be kind of funny that Mathew was sleeping with anyone, let alone Bette. But then, when he heard the bed creak, and Bette let out a soft moan, his sense of humor deserted him.

He wasn't thinking clearly. He walked back up the stairs and went into his room and sat down on the side of his bed. He sat until six a.m., then he heard her quietly open and shut Mathew's door and tip-toe across the hall. When she came into his room, wearing her pink nightgown, she didn't look the least bit surprised to see him.

"What the hell are you doing?" he said.

She didn't say anything for a while. She just stood looking at him, thinking. Her arms hanging down at her sides, her bare feet planted solidly on the rug. Finally she shook her head and shrugged. "I guess I'm leaving," she said and she began to move around the room picking things up off the floor, pulling her shorts on, stuffing clothing in her suitcase.

"You fucking slept with him," he managed to get out. It took all his power not to get up off the bed and start throwing things.

She stopped what she was doing and turned to him. "I realize, Henry. You don't need to tell me." Then she zipped up her suitcase and wheeled it out of the room. The wheels were whining, like a kid crying out. He heard her go into the bathroom and then a few minutes later she went down the stairs, obviously struggling with the suitcase. He stood up and paced around the room. He felt crazed but he wasn't sure what to do about it. He sat back down and a little while later her car started with a roar, backed out of the driveway, and was gone.

What was a relief was not the sex part of it but allowing himself to feel how he'd felt for her from the start. Mathew could see it now. Since he'd met her on the stairs that night with Henry, he'd seen something in her that had made him practically weak with desire. Not that he told her this. In fact she basically did all of the talking, but he didn't mind it. He lay next to her and felt her warm sweet-smelling breath on his chest as she talked, and he felt better than he could ever remember feeling. Not happy but good, in a way that made his blood warm and free-flowing throughout his body and made his mind work smoothly, taking in all the good and bad things around him but not getting tripped up as he usually did.

After she'd tiptoed out of his room that Sunday morning, he'd fallen right off to sleep and he slept until ten o'clock. When he looked out the window he saw it was a dark day, on the verge of rain, and he noticed his car windows were down. So he put on his slippers and a tee-shirt and went downstairs. His head was still murky from sleep. He walked across the porch and down to the lawn and was heading through the deep grass to his car.

It all happened so fast that there wasn't time to think. First there was a sort of crying, then a second later the pounding of footsteps. He turned just in time to see Henry charging at him across the grass. His brother looked frantic, his face soaked with tears, his eyes opened wide with an expression of horror. Mathew knew what was next. None of it surprised him really, the fact that Henry landed on him and suddenly they were on the ground. Even Henry's fists pummeling his body and his head he felt somehow prepared for. The only thing that came as a surprise was his brother's sobbing. A terrible kind of wailing that felt more painful than any of the punches, making him instantly heartsick and causing him to lie still and let Henry pound away.

When I heard them out on the lawn it took me long full minutes to realize something was wrong. That breathy punching and grunting and a small yelping that made me think at first a dog had been hit out on the road. But then I realized what it was, even before I went to the window and looked down.

There they were, rolling around in a clump on the lawn, and I could see Henry's fists hitting Mathew frantically. It felt like I was running down the stairs before I even opened the door to my room. I was moving so fast that, for a long time later, my unused muscles were too sore to touch. I must have looked wild coming across the porch in my nightgown, moving in large thunderous footsteps down to the tall grass of the lawn, silent as one of those big cats going after their prey, silent and swift. I was on top of them a second later and I landed with such force that I think I scared the wits out of Henry.

I grabbed the first thing I could, which was a fistful of his thick hair, and I pulled and I said, "You stop it."

He was crying, sobbing hysterically. He rolled over in a ball in the grass and held on to himself and cried all out.

Mathew was on his back, staring at him, blinking, his face covered with blood and blood coming out of his nose like a fountain. "Can you stand up?" I said. He nodded and looked at me. I helped him get up and he limped slowly into the house. I made him sit down on the couch in the study and I propped his head back with a couple of pillows. Then I was in the bathroom soaking a towel with cold water and wringing it out.

I thought I was going to have to drive him to the hospital but I didn't think he needed it once the blood slowed. It wasn't until later, when I saw his nose had been broken, that I realized he probably should have been taken to the emergency room.

"See if Henry's okay, Mom," he said in a hoarse voice.

I got up off the couch and went back out onto the porch but Henry was gone. There was only a patch of dented-down grass where they'd been fighting. "Henry," I said in a voice only loud enough for someone standing close by to hear. I stood still and a breeze came up through the trees and made my nightgown flutter around my feet. It felt like rain, the sky dark and that aluminum smell in the air. It was the first time I'd been outside all summer long. I felt dazed and overcome. Like someone who'd survived a plane wreck in the middle of nowhere and suddenly found herself rescued, back home with everything the way it had been but not one thing the same.

Chapter 11

After his mother led Mathew into the house, Henry started to run. He quit crying and just poured himself into the air, pumping his arms and making his legs extend out in front of him. He ran into the woods, leaping over stone walls and fallen trees, plowing straight through whole herds of brambles. He stopped thinking about everything and just ran until he was deep in the woods. Swallowed by the trees. So far out that he could no longer hear the sounds of lawn mowers or traffic along the road. There was just his own hard breathing and a few lone birds whistling out.

He ran all the way up to the old Wolf Hill Boy Scout Camp, about four miles from the house. He was surprised when he suddenly burst into the clearing and found himself there. It was a place abandoned now for some time, a place his father had taken him for overnight camping trips.

He wound up staying there three days. Sleeping curled up on the dirt floor of a cabin. When he'd wake everything would come back to him in a rush and he'd feel a kind of fresh horror about Mathew and Bette. About her leaving. About his father vanishing from his life the way he had. But after a while the quiet of the woods started to seep into him and he seemed to come back to himself. Regain a kind of balance.

On the second day he went through several bad hours thinking he should do himself in. He wasn't sure what he was sticking around for. But the idea of being gone made him sad anyway, not necessarily because he'd miss anyone but because he couldn't help thinking he'd sort of miss himself. His own face and his stupid jokes and the junkyard of thoughts in his head.

Not that his visions of the future were anything but dismal. Yet by the third day, as he began to walk back towards the house with his stomach brutally empty and his mind brutally clear, he'd made himself a kind of strict plan to stick to for a while. A sort of map leading nowhere but at least, he figured, leading on.

It was probably the first day they'd brought him home. A tiny little red thing wrapped in a blue blanket. A scrunched-up face. "This is Henry, your new brother," his mother had said. She put him down in a crib and then she went into the bathroom. Mathew stood next to the crib for a minute and listened to him breathing. The house had been peaceful up until then, just him and his parents. He looked at his new brother's miniature hands curled into soft fists and his little closed eyelids. He thought about it for a second, looked around to make sure the coast was clear, then reached in and grabbed a fingerful of skin and pinched with such might he bit his own tongue in the process. Then the screaming started. Like an air raid siren filling the room, causing his mother to race from the bathroom half dressed. "Did you touch him!? What did you do to him!?" He stepped back and shook his head, but by the next day a circular blue bruise appeared on the side of his brother's face, like a sad initiation mark into his new home.

The memory started to haunt Mathew that fall. Up until then he'd tucked it neatly away in his mind, but it kept coming back to him, clear and cruel. He couldn't remember ever laying a hand on Henry after that. But he had done the next worst thing, he'd simply made like he wasn't there. He ignored him. Slammed doors in his face. Walked silently past him in the hallway. Left the room when he entered. Then to top it all off he'd slept with Bette, unable to control himself when she slid into bed beside him.

He spent the next three days up in his room, rotating his ice pack from his broken nose to his eye and back to his nose. He kept the shade pulled down and looked up at the ceiling. He couldn't remember ever feeling so depressed. Not only because the house was suddenly, dreadfully quiet with Bette gone but because for the first time he started to look at himself. Started to remember his life as a kid. And what had always felt like an innocent need for privacy and quiet now looked more like a vicious way of punishing someone for just being born.

Henry came back three days after having vanished. Mathew was on his way down the stairs for a fresh ice pack when his brother appeared at the bottom. He was almost unrecognizable. His hair hung in strands across his face and a patchy beard had grown in around his chin, making him look like the kind of people Mathew had seen walking alongside freeways, or asking for money on the street in Boston. Mathew froze on the step and tried to come up with something to say but Henry didn't even seem to see him. He just climbed the stairs, looking down at his mud-caked feet, and walked right past him into his room, quietly shutting the door.

And despite feeling sorry for Henry, the thing that tortured Mathew the most was how much he missed Bette. More than missed her really. He ached for her. And not necessarily for her in his bed; it was more her voice that he missed, the same voice that reminded him at first of a dentist's drill. And the smell of her gum. And the shoes left where he was always tripping over them. And the roar of her lousy car and the black cloud of toxic fumes lingering in the driveway every day after she drove off to work.

The school bus went by the house at seven-thirty every morning. It came grinding up the hill and I'd wake to the sound of all those kids inside, hollering and laughing, rattling the quiet of the morning as it roared by. I was pure heartbeat after it was gone. My whole body booming away. It was fall now. Life was going on.

Henry reappeared after four days. He came into my room and caught me sitting at my desk writing in a notebook, smoking a cigarette. I practically didn't recognize him. His hair was gone. He'd cut it so short he looked like a marine. He came in and stood in the middle of the room and said, "I don't think you really care, Mom, but I'm not going to go back to school. I can't. I'm going to work until I have enough money to move out."

Before I had time to think of anything to say he turned, walked out of the room, and shut the door firmly behind him. And that was pretty much the last I saw of him for a while. The back of his tightly cropped skull as he left the room.

He'd come and go quietly, usually entering the house through the front door and going right up the stairs to his room.

I guess I could have fought him, but I didn't want to anymore.

So I'd get up in the mornings and put my old clothes on and look in the mirror, and it was just strange seeing me there, my skin tenting over my cheekbones. And I'd get the feeling looking at myself that I'd walked out and never come back. Just walked clear out, with the door banging shut behind me and the sound of my feet going out across the porch.

Part Two

Chapter 12

Some people wanted their leaves raked every week. Others wanted them raked only once when they'd all come down off the trees. It was harder work than mowing. At night Henry's back ached and his arms seemed to stay sore. But it was quieter work, no big engines roaring around him, just the rhythmic sound of the bamboo clawing the ground. For some reason he did less thinking about things while he was raking, and he preferred it this way.

When he went to get his job back he told Jeff there was one condition if he was going to work for him again and that was that he wasn't going to smoke pot anymore. Jeff got defensive at the time. "Christ, Iris, I don't give a shit if you smoke or not, that's your business. What, like I was pressuring you or something?"

"Not at all," Henry said. "I just wanted to let you know I'm quitting for a while."

"Then quit for crying out loud, don't tell me about it!" Jeff went red in the face. But he didn't mention it again and he quit smoking in front of Henry altogether, even though he still showed up stoned in the mornings.

After they were done working most nights they'd stop by Cubby's, the town's only bar, and have a couple of beers, Henry's daily limit. The place was filled with townies, guys who worked for the highway department, all smelling of creosote and chugging down pitchers of beer. Now that it was fall everything took on a serious feeling, like this was just life. No more high school. There was something depressing about it. Henry started to feel as if everyone around him had gotten stuck somehow, stuck in the town, stuck in their lives. It occurred to him the same thing could happen to him.

It was Jeff who pointed out that one of the waitresses, a girl named Janeen who was a few years older than Henry, had a crush on him. That was how he started going out with her, because Jeff pointed her out. Otherwise, he figured, he wouldn't have even noticed. Not that she wasn't attractive—she had a lot of frizzy brown hair and nice green eyes—but he hadn't been looking.

She had an apartment above the A & P in town and the first time after they made love Henry lay on his back and felt like he was sinking down through the mattress. He couldn't stop thinking about Bette. "Are you all right?" Janeen whispered.

"Oh, yeah," he said. "Sorry, I just started falling asleep."

He reached out and touched her face. That night he could hear the freezers in the store below them going on and off like big animals sighing and yawning down in the dark. He closed his eyes and went over the lyrics of "Mr. Tambourine Man" as a way of moving his mind somewhere else.

After a couple of weeks she gave him the key to her apartment, which he gladly took. Not because he longed for her exactly, more because it meant he didn't have to go back to his house every night. After work he'd go from the bar over to the IGA, where he'd buy a sandwich in the deli. Then he'd go upstairs to her place, sit on her bed, watch TV, and wait for her to come back from work. And sometimes without really thinking about it he'd get up and go over to the window and stand there scanning the rows of cars in the parking lot, hoping for some ridiculous reason that he'd see Bette's white Nova down there.

Mathew left his bedroom door open at night now, mostly to relieve his loneliness, which burdened him. He'd sit at his old desk and study the vegetarian cookbook Bette had left behind, deciding which recipes he'd try the next day, making a grocery list of the ingredients he would need. Ever since his nose had been broken, his glasses sat lopsided on his face, like a horse's saddle might sit on the bony back of a cow. And they were covered with dried pieces of dill and splatterings of tomato sauce, smeared at the edges from his greasy fingers.

It had taken him a couple of weeks to find the cookbook. Not that it had been hidden. In fact she'd left it right out on the kitchen counter where he'd had to move it several times to clean. It just took him that long to see it. Up until then he hadn't found a trace of her anywhere in the house (with the exception of a few long blond hairs on his pillow). She seemed thoroughly gone. Vanished. Then he discovered the book right there in front of him one afternoon and when he opened to some of its turned-down pages he recognized the recipes from those last meals with her.

Before that first day with the cookbook he'd never followed a recipe in his life. He'd never sautéed garlic on a medium flame or chopped herbs or pureed soup in a blender. It was a whole new world, and now that he stepped into it he was surprised to find it suited him.

He cooked three meals a day, each of which his mother would dress for, in the clothes he remembered seeing on her all his life, her blue jean skirt and sneakers, her cotton button-down shirts. It wasn't that she was back to normal; in fact she'd changed so much he wasn't quite sure who she was or how to act around her. She still didn't leave the house except occasionally after dinner to go out and stroll around the overgrown lawn, still didn't do any laundry or dishes or vacuuming. She'd started smoking cigarettes, writing in a journal, watching television with an abandon that made him uncomfortable.

Sometimes he had the urge to ask her just what it was she was doing. He wanted to say, "How long is this all going to last?" But the fact was that she could ask him the same question and he'd probably have the same answer: "I don't know."

It occurred to him that they were both recuperating. She from a life that had pretty much led her nowhere, and he, when he gave it some thought, from just about the same thing.

Maybe if we were starving something would have kicked in. Some will or instinct of some kind. Maybe then I would have walked back into the world. Gotten a job. But as it was I didn't seem to have any kind of calling. Even to be a mother. It was no longer there. It hadn't done anyone a whole lot of good when I played the part to begin with. When I fought all those years to bring Mathew out of his shell. When I wept wildly every time Henry was suspended from school. Life had just taken its course. With me thrashing alongside the whole time.

Just like with Gordie. All those meals and shirts ironed and he'd gone and left anyway.

It was a relief partly, simply to acknowledge how futile all the struggling had been, and to let it go. It had been exhausting. I don't remember a single night when I didn't climb into bed thoroughly tired and depleted.

Not that it was clear what was left.

On the first page of the little notebook I made Mathew buy for me I wrote my name, Augusta, in small, perfectly executed letters. Then I sat there and stared at it and smoked close to a whole pack of cigarettes before I shut the book and went downstairs for dinner.

And that was the craziest thing of all. That there was Mathew, with his hair now down to his shoulders, whistling under his breath and cooking one glorious meal after the other. Not because I'd pushed him into it but the opposite obviously, because I'd quit.

They'd run out of lawns that afternoon, and after sitting in front of the supermarket eating yet another meatball grinder for lunch (he didn't feel comfortable hanging around Janeen's apartment during the day, he got the feeling he was in her way), Henry wound up kicking around town, wandering with his hands in his pockets past the library and the elementary school and the town hall. It was mid-October now and it was starting to get cold out. He'd yet to make a trip up to his house for his down jacket and warmer shirts, so he wore only his sweatshirt, which leaked the wind right through. It was because he was so cold that he wound up walking into the congregational church and sitting down in one of the pews, for a long time just staring out in front of him at the altar and the stained-glass windows. He felt a little uneasy being there, seeing that he wasn't religious, but he didn't want to leave. The place was heated, and it was also peaceful and dark.

There was also something about it that made him want to let down his guard and just be truthful. Truthful with himself about how he'd been feeling for a long time, which was nothing but sad, in through his bones and blood and all around him. His whole life had come unraveled and he just wasn't at all sure anymore what was left.

Eventually he lay down across a pew; he lay on his side with his hood on and his feet tucked up towards him and his hands under his face and he shut his eyes and after a while he fell deeply asleep, his mouth dropping open, his breath leaving him in long slow waves.

When Henry woke up, there was a man standing in the aisle looking down at him. He was wearing a red down ski jacket and holding a large cardboard box. "I'm sorry," the man said. "I didn't mean to wake you. Looks like you're pooped."

Henry sat up and rubbed his face hard. He felt out of it. The nap had taken him clear away from the day. "I'm real sorry, I didn't mean to—sorry." He stood up and made his way into the aisle. "Just came in here to look around, sorry." He turned and started towards the doors. He felt humiliated.

"That's why the doors are open, Henry," he heard the man say behind him, and it then dawned on him this was the same guy he'd met in the pharmacy during the summer.

"Anybody can come in here. For whatever reason," Reverend Desell said.

Henry turned around. "Welp, thanks, but I better get going." He was backing away now, trying not to be rude.

"Listen, Henry, I do hope you don't mind my asking again how your mother is." The reverend set his cardboard box on one of the benches and unzipped his jacket.

Henry was ready to say what he'd been saying for months to this question, that she was fine, away on a trip, but he felt exhausted suddenly. He looked at the reverend's face, at his red nose and his eyes tearing from the wind outside, and he finally shook his head.

"I see," the reverend said. "Not so good, I gather."

Henry stared down at the floor. He felt he couldn't put up a front for anyone anymore. It was as if there were now a part of him running ahead waving a white flag, surrendering.

"How 'bout you come back to my office for a cup of tea, or coffee, and we talk a little bit."

"I'm not religious," Henry blurted out. "I mean, shouldn't I be? Aren't I supposed to be religious if you're going to talk to me?"

"Please." The reverend waved his hand. "Let's just go have a chat and maybe, or maybe not, we can work out a few things here."

He started down the aisle to the front and Henry, after hesitating a moment, not knowing what else to do, followed. He was wondering screen was a middle-aged woman. She had tightly cropped gray hair and an impatient look on her face.

Before he could say anything she said, "Are you one of the Iris boys?"

"Uhm, yes, I am."

"Well, I am Madeline Westford, the postmistress, and I am here to tell you that if you don't come pick up your mail we are going to have no choice but to send everything back."

"Mail?"

"I highly recommend you get in your car no later than five this afternoon and come pick it up." She turned and walked across the porch. Mathew stood with his doughed-up hands suspended in the air as her heels hammered down the walk to her car. He felt deflated. Since he never got letters, it never occurred to him to get the mail.

Although he was reluctant to leave the house now since he had a full afternoon of chores and cooking ahead of him, after he was finished with the crust he wrapped it up and stuck it in the freezer, removed his apron, and headed out to his car.

He imagined that there'd be a small pile, but the amount he found in the back room of the post office shocked him. "Oh," he said when the woman pointed out the postal bag.

As he went to pick it up he felt his back twinge.

"Charlie!" the woman yelled over her shoulder. "When you have a minute, can you help him lift this?"

A minute later a man showed up. Mathew was expecting some big hulking type but Charlie was as wiry as he was and the two of them grunted and strained all the way out to Mathew's car. He gave

Mathew the thumbs-up sign once they'd thrown the bag into the trunk.

"Sorry 'bout this," Mathew said.

The man shrugged. "Hey, no problem, it's given us something to talk about."

"Oh," Mathew said, and climbed into his car. He rolled down the window and thanked the man, then drove home. He felt shaken up. The whole experience was both humiliating and irritating. Didn't they have anything better to do than discuss his family?

That night when his mother came down for dinner, she stopped at the mountain of mail he'd dumped onto the living room floor. "What's this?"

Mathew came out of the kitchen and saw her standing there. She looked worried. "Our mail," he said. "We sort of forgot about it."

His mother said, "Oh dear." She stepped gingerly around the pile, like it was a drunk passed out on the floor, blocking her way.

After dinner, when she'd gone back upstairs and Mathew heard the TV go on, he sat down cross-legged on the rug and started to sort. There were piles of bills, piles of warnings—first warnings, second warnings, last warnings. Nobody had paid. Not for lack of money, because also in the pile were statements from his parents' joint bank account and there was plenty, for a while anyway. There was his father's mail as well—letters and gallery openings and magazines.

Then there was the pile of blue airmail letters to his mother from his father in England. He'd seen them right off when he'd emptied the mail bag and he had a feeling his mother had seen them too, or just sensed them in the pile. There were eighteen airmail letters all him reach out and touch the door. Henry's sculpture. Really nothing more than a big jumble of junk, but there was something about the way everything clung together, the way old tires and the hand of a mannequin and a rusty-looking typewriter seemed to suspend themselves in the air that brought a sudden and powerful lump into Mathew's throat. Maybe just from the surprise of seeing it there. Or maybe because it struck him that it was born out of his brother's agony, then left alone in the musty room in a kind of sad, graceful limbo.

"**Do** you think I can come up there?" He was standing down in the driveway with his hands in his jacket pockets. I hadn't seen him in five days and I'd run out of cigarettes. I realized he only came by when Mathew was out, and Mathew hadn't gone out for several days this time. "If you don't want me to I understand, but I just . . ."

"Come up. Go around the front and just come up the stairs."

It's true I didn't want him to come up, but I just couldn't take all those cigarettes from him and then tell him he wasn't welcome. So I watched him walk around the house and a minute later I heard him on the stairs. He stopped at the top of them and I got up and opened my door.

"You sure you don't mind?" he said. "I respect your need for privacy."

He was taller than he looked from above. "You look different," I said.

With his left hand he produced a pack of cigarettes from his pocket. He handed them to me, then said, "Well, anyway, I'll go."

"Come in," I told him.

He put his hands back into his jacket and stood there for a second. "Okay," he said. He smelled of cold weather and outdoors. He stopped in the middle of the room and looked around. "Huh," he said.

"What?"

"Well, funnily enough, this is sort of how I imagined it would be. That's rare, you know, when a place lives up to your imagination."

He walked over and sat down in the chair in the corner and put his hands on his knees. He let out a deep breath. "I'm sorry, I guess you must think I'm pretty off."

I sat down on the side of my bed and said, "You must think I am."

"Maybe we're both a little off." He looked up and we caught eyes and there was a glint of pleasure in his.

Then I glanced down at my feet. Where I always look when words fail me.

"Smoke?" he said, and when I looked up he had a cigarette dangling out of his mouth and he was holding one out to me.

"And how." I laughed and took it from him.

"You want to know something, Mrs. Iris?"

"Don't call me that please. It makes me feel like a spinster. My name is Augusta."

"All right, Augusta. You want to know something?"

"Okay."

"Well, last June I saw your husband with Marion over in Clark's Corners. I was over there getting my mowers sharpened and while I was waiting I went into the little diner there and I saw the two of them sitting at a booth together."

"Did you."

"I knew who he was and I knew who you were and I knew you weren't her. If you know what I mean."

I nodded.

"Anyway, then a few weeks after that I was down at the supermarket and I parked my truck next to your car. And as I was getting out I saw you inside, lying there across the front seat."

"Oh dear."

"You see, I didn't know what to do. I knew what was going on and I guessed why you were lying there but I didn't know what I should do about it. I got back into my truck and sat there for a while and thought about it. Then I got out and knocked on your window."

"I heard you knocking."

"You remember that?"

"I do remember, actually."

"Then I went in and called Henry and when I came back out there was a whole group of people standing around your car. Then Henry came."

"And took me home."

He nodded.

"And here I've been." I motioned to the room.

"Yeah, well," he said.

I looked at him. The place was filled with cigarette smoke. I remembered him, back in my other life. We would pass each other walking out of the hardware store or the pharmacy, his long hair and his beat-up army jacket, his truck. Like two lone planets from wholly different galaxies rolling on by each other.

That Saturday night, sleeping beside Janeen, Henry dreamed his father was floating facedown on the town pond, his body bobbing across the water. He woke up with a jolt and it took him a minute to remember where he was. It was as if he were peeling away his past to get to where he was at that moment. Not home, not with Bette, no longer in school; it was no longer summer. He got out of bed and went into the bathroom and turned the light on. After looking at himself in the mirror for a while, seeing his sleep-ridden face and his hair sticking up in the back, he went and sat down on the side of the tub.

He had spent that evening watching a football game at the bar while Janeen worked. He drank two beers, and at eleven when Janeen got off, he went home with her. The only thing he couldn't do was make love. He tried for a couple of minutes when they first got into bed but then, as he told her, he was just too exhausted and it wasn't that he didn't want to, he just couldn't seem to. The fact was that ever since he'd seen Bette's car drive by a few days earlier and ever since he'd told the reverend that he was waiting to be forgiven, he felt different. Not necessarily better, just a little less like he was lying to himself.

Now he sat on the side of the tub and looked down at the cold tile floor. The dream had made him ache all over. Not only the horror of

Mathew was doing the dishes that Sunday morning, when he heard a knock at the back door. He sighed irritably, shut off the water, and wiped his hands on a dish towel. He wondered who would show up this early on a Sunday. Some kind of church type, he figured.

When he got to the door he was surprised to see him standing outside, his shoulders hunched up as usual, his hands crammed into his jacket pockets. There was a large black garbage bag sitting on the ground beside him. Mathew opened the door. "Henry? What are you doing?"

"Sort of freezing," Henry said.

It was the first time Mathew had seen him since several weeks back in the supermarket.

"Well, why are you knocking? Why don't you just come inside?"

Henry shrugged. "I guess I kind of thought before I did we should get some stuff out in the open."

"Oh," Mathew said. He felt a dipping inside. "Well, okay, let me just get my coat on. It's freezing out. You sure you just don't want to step inside? We can talk right here in the doorway."

Henry shook his head. "No. If you don't mind. I'm trying—"

"All right." Mathew cut him off. "Hang on, I'll be right back."

He quickly walked into the coatroom and found one of his father's old down jackets hanging on a hook. As he slipped into it he noticed his hands were shaking. He couldn't help feeling Henry might punch him out again.

Henry was where he had left him. Still hunched up and shivering. It was a dark day out and the first thing Mathew thought as he stepped into the air was snow. He could just smell it gathering up in the sky, about to start falling.

"Sorry to make you stand out here," Henry said.

"That's okay." Mathew watched a white cloud of breath leave his mouth.

"I've been living with this girl downtown." Henry gave a small sigh; he looked down. "But I, uh, she . . . well, I guess I was kind of using her, I mean so I wouldn't have to stay here."

Mathew nodded sadly.

"I've been kind of upset." Henry's words came out slowly and after he said them they seemed to sit there on air, half filled with anger and half in a kind of surrender.

"Yeah," Mathew said. He too had started to look at the ground. He still thought Henry might hit him. But he didn't care anymore. "I understand, Henry," he was whispering.

"I mean, I guess I've been upset 'cause you slept with her but . . ."

When Mathew heard this he suddenly reached up and covered his face with a hand; he shook his head. "I can't stand it." He was talking so low he almost didn't even hear himself. "I just can't stand it, I just wish I could go back and change everything, I just keep wishing. . . ."

"Well," Henry said. "What can we do about it? I mean, I sort of wish certain things too but it doesn't do anybody any good. I think we better just get on with it."

Mathew took his hand away from his face. He shook his head again. "I didn't mean to hurt you, Henry. I just don't even think I was thinking. But I know, that seems to be the way it's always been."

"Well." Henry shrugged and smiled. "So."

"But I'm so sorry." They were words he'd needed to get out and once they did he felt uncorked, unable to control himself. He put his face back into his hands. He then felt Henry's hand drop down on his shoulder.

"Well, guess what," he heard his brother say. "Guess what?" And he felt Henry lean closer to him. "I forgive you."

When Mathew finally took his hands away from his face, he saw that snow had started coming down in ridiculously large slow-falling flakes and through his blurred eyes he saw Henry looking at him with his arms crossed over his chest, grinning, like he'd just accomplished a major feat.

Chapter 14

I woke up around eight o'clock on Thanksgiving morning and right off it was clear that Mathew had been roasting the turkey for at least an hour already. The house was fat with its smell. I lay still. Then I thought, Okay, get up, but I didn't move.

They both came into my room eventually. First Mathew; then he went out and sent Henry in.

"I just can't," I told each of them.

It was Henry who went downstairs and made the call. I heard his voice on the phone but I didn't know who he was calling. I didn't care. I was wrapped up in that smell; it lay on top of me like a brick blanket.

Around noon it was Jeff who knocked at my door, then gently pushed it open. I blinked over at him. He had his hair combed and pulled back into a ponytail and was wearing a sports jacket. He looked awkward cleaned up. The way a dairy farmer might look at church.

"Mind if I come in?"

"Come in," I said.

He shut the door behind him. It had gotten quiet in the house. I knew both Mathew and Henry were down in the kitchen. All the clanking around of pots and pans I had heard earlier had stopped. They were now waiting.

He was wearing different shoes, quieter than his usual boots when he walked across the floor. When he sat down in the chair in the corner, I saw they were those old-fashioned kind of sneakers. The boating kind. They'd been white once.

He sighed but didn't say anything until I looked at him. Then he said, "Henry called me, actually."

I nodded.

"They've got this big meal down there. Looks good. Looks better than the one over at my house. My mom cooks a chicken because she says a turkey's too much food for three people. Chicken, mashed yams and string beans, and a pumpkin pie for dessert. That's our Thanksgiving. I mean, she used to do the whole thing, but I don't know, I guess once I wasn't a kid anymore she didn't see the point."

He stopped. He was leaning forward, his elbows on his knees and his hands clasped together. He was thinking. After a while he looked at me and said, "I guess you've always made a big meal for everyone?"

I looked at him.

"Turkey?"

I nodded.

"Did you make turnips?"

"Mashed turnips." I smiled.

"Oh, I love that stuff. How 'bout that cranberry sauce, did you use the cans or make your own?"

"I'd make my own if I could find the cranberries."

"It's a good holiday, isn't it? Just a food holiday, not a whole hell of a lot more than that. You know, no big God issues at stake. Just a big meal."

"I appreciate your trying," I said quietly.

"But I'm not a shrink, I realize." There was a long silence before he went on. "I know it's weird. I mean the fact that I keep coming around here. I know both Mathew and Henry are pretty baffled about the whole thing"—he was talking to the floor now—"but for some reason, don't ask me why, I feel like I understand you, Augusta." He paused then and said, "You don't have to get up if you don't want . . ."

I closed my eyes. My insides hurt. My life was over. The fact that it was Thanksgiving and I wasn't downstairs whipping cream for the pie or telling Henry to quit vulturing must mean that my life was somehow over, even if I wasn't dead yet.

I heard him stand up and a second later he sat down beside me on the mattress, his weight making my body fall a little towards him. I kept my eyes closed. I heard his breathing. Then I felt the back of his hand touch my face. It was cool and it smelled musty, like cigarettes. I hadn't been touched for so long by another person that the sensation literally went through me like electricity and made me jump. I opened my eyes and he was sitting there, looking at me like a big question mark. I looked into his eyes. There was something sad in them. Lonesome. After a while I said, "Okay."

"Okay." He looked relieved. "I'll wait for you on the stairs while you get dressed. Is that all right?"

His hand was still there, touching my face. "Okay," I said.

At first it was just another thing for Henry to feel angry about. Another reason not to want to live at home. Several days before Thanksgiving, when his mother mentioned to him and Mathew that Jeff Truly had become a friend of hers, it took everything in him to keep from going ape. First he wanted to shake her for being so ridiculous. Next he wanted to punch Jeff out for putting the moves on her. But he just sat there with his face sewn up and looked out the kitchen window while she told them both. She still wasn't strong enough to have him yelling at her. She was still in this weird, fragile, otherworldly state.

When she went upstairs he said to Mathew, "I can't fucking believe it. I mean I've been checking out girls with this guy all summer and now he's making the moves on Mom?! Christ!"

Mathew shook his head, then stood up and opened the fridge. Henry could tell his brother wasn't as upset as he was. "I mean, do you realize this guy is thirty-five years old?" Henry said. "I mean, how old is Mom, forty-five, forty-eight?"

"Uhm," Mathew said. Henry heard him shifting things around in the fridge. "Uh, I actually don't even know. Jesus, that's not very good, is it?"

"Anyway . . ." Henry could tell Mathew was trying to get him off the subject of Jeff. "It's disgusting. Man. I swear I'm going to say something."

Mathew shut the fridge door. He was holding a big glass bowl with some sort of brown liquid in it. He sighed and brought it over to the counter. "Well, maybe you should just wait and see."

"Wait and see what?"

"Well, I just get the feeling that maybe we shouldn't keep anyone away from her. What harm could it do? She said they're just friends." He was peering into the bowl, sniffing the contents. "I figure it's better she see somebody, anybody practically, rather than nobody."

Henry looked back out the window. He pictured Jeff in his head, raunchy, smoking pot. "She's really flipped out," he said quietly. "I mean, she's definitely nutso now."

Then three days later, on Thanksgiving, she had that same look on her face that she'd had all summer. Like she was awake but she wasn't really there. It made Henry panic.

Mathew was at the kitchen table looking thoroughly despondent. "No luck, huh?" he said when Henry walked in. The kitchen was in a kind of halted chaos, the sink filled with pots and pans, a bowl of half-mashed sweet potatoes still dimly steaming next to the stove, and the turkey sputtering away in the oven. Henry stood there drumming his fingers on the counter. Thinking how they had to get her up, how they couldn't start over again with her back in bed. He took a big breath and let it go slowly; then he turned and picked up the phone.

"It's Henry," he said when Jeff came on. They hadn't seen each other for a couple of weeks now.

"Oh." Jeff sounded apologetic. Henry could tell right off how uncomfortable he was, too.

"We're making this big meal and she won't get out of bed."

There was a long silence. When Jeff finally spoke he seemed to be talking under his breath, as if he didn't want someone nearby to hear him. "Can I come over?"

"I guess," Henry said, and hung up the phone. He might need his help, he thought, but that didn't mean he had to be friendly to the guy.

Jeff arrived about fifteen minutes later, looking plagued with embarrassment. Mathew greeted him at the door while Henry, still at the table, only grunted. Mathew brought Jeff through the kitchen and to the bottom of the stairs, then came back and sat down next to Henry.

"Sometimes you got to just tell yourself to let go of things," Mathew said quietly. "Like you did with me. You got to just tell yourself to let it go."

Henry looked at his brother. He suddenly realized Mathew was angry at him. His face was red with it.

"Otherwise there isn't any room in this world for anybody but you."

Mathew stood up and went over to the bowl of sweet potatoes and started mashing them.

Henry put his head down on the table so that his cheek was resting on the cool wood. His chest was aching. He was thinking about Bette the way he did now every time he started to feel bad. Like his blood was whispering to her, a language he knew only she could make out. But Mathew was right: he shut people out, and once they were out he was that much more alone. There he was, expecting everyone around him to behave a certain way, when in fact he acted worse than anyone.

About an hour later his mom and Jeff appeared in the kitchen.

They weren't actually touching each other but somehow when Henry looked up they seemed attached, allied, the way people get after they've been through something together. It surprised him.

All four of them seemed to pause and there was a moment when no one was quite sure what to do next. Then Henry stood up, opened the refrigerator door, got a beer out, and handed it to Jeff.

Jeff unscrewed the cap and the only sound in the kitchen was the gasp of air escaping from the bottle. Like the sound a swimmer makes when he comes up out of deep water.

That night after he and Henry cleaned up the kitchen, Mathew put on his father's old down jacket and took a walk out to the end of the road. Having spent the entire day inside, cooking and eating, he was badly in need of air. It was only six o'clock but it was pitch-black out and so cold everything seemed to be holding deeply still. At one point he tipped back his head and was surprised to see the vast ocean of stars above him. He hadn't thought about stars in so long. Even when he was studying them they had stopped being stars and started being other things, molecules millions of miles away. It was like Bette had said: if you look at things too closely, you stop seeing them for what they are. It felt good to look at them the way he once saw them as a kid, out of reach, shimmering, just the very thought of them boggling the mind.

He walked down to the end of the road, then turned and started back. It was cold and as he put his hands into his jacket pockets he felt something soft and round inside. He stopped and pulled it out and blinked at it in the darkness. He couldn't quite make it out with his eyes but he knew what it was. He had felt it right off. The old rabbit's foot that his father used to carry with him all the time. Mathew hadn't seen it in years. He stuck it back into his pocket but as he walked home his hand kept turning it, smoothing the fur with a thumb. He was wondering what made his father stop keeping it with him.

Henry was reading the classifieds in the kitchen when he walked back in. Mathew stood in the door and said, "Here. Catch."

Henry lifted his head, and his hand went out in time to snatch the rabbit's foot out of the air. He opened his palm and looked at it. "Holy shit," he muttered.

Mathew watched his brother's face. It went from surprise to sadness. "I'd forgotten all about that thing," Henry said, and tossed it back across the kitchen to Mathew.

"Me too," he said after he caught it and slipped it back into his pocket. "Forgot all about it."

He'd gone to Yale. Three years of it, studying natural resources and then, he said, it went out of him. Or maybe more, he said, he realized he'd never had it in him to begin with and he came home, back to his room and his two quiet parents. Back to this town. That was sixteen years ago. And he'd lived in that same room since. Mowing lawns in the summer. Selling a little pot in the winter. Reading spy novels by the hundreds.

He told me all this Thanksgiving night. We were in my room smoking cigarettes and he unfolded himself for me. "A fuckup," he said, "but a high-thinking one."

I looked at his sneakers and felt a flush of warmth for him. An outsider, I thought. Lonely enough to come after me.

.

Chapter 15

Henry and Jeff spent the morning getting Augusta's car running again. They had to change the one flat tire, clean the windshield off (which was no easy chore since it had been sitting under a maple tree for months without moving), and then they had to jump-start it and take it for a drive to recharge the battery. It was December and Jeff sat in the passenger seat and kept fiddling with the defrost. Henry drove through town; then they decided they should drive to Madly and back to give the battery more juice. Even though they'd spent time together they hadn't really been alone together the way you are in a car, and Henry felt a little nervous. Suddenly he wasn't quite sure what to say. But Jeff was the one who started talking.

"So my parents keep bugging me that they want to meet my new girlfriend."

Henry glanced over at Jeff and saw that he was looking through the windshield with an amused expression on his face.

Henry smiled. "Welp, bring them on over."

"Yeah, right. I can just see my mom's expression. Shock to horror, then trying to look pleased. Christ, I don't look forward to that one."

There was a moment of quiet, just the sound of the blinker as Henry turned the car onto Madly-Rumkin Road. Henry said, "I mean . . . I keep wanting to ask you something."

"Go ahead and ask."

"Welp. What's the deal anyway? How come you . . ."

"How come I'm hanging around with your mom, right?"

"Well, yeah."

"Because I like her. I mean, that's really the reason. I think at first I felt bad for her. You know, I kept hearing you tell me about her this summer and I felt sorry for her. But then when I met her I didn't feel all that sorry for her. I just liked her. She's different."

Henry shook his head.

"I know, man." Jeff looked at him. "You don't need to tell me how weird it is. I know. I wake up at night and I sort of can't believe it, you know it kind of strikes me fresh. But, you know, I . . ." He blew out a big breath. "I appreciate how accepting you've been. I know it hasn't been easy."

"It's been fucking weird, that's what it's been." Henry shrugged. "But I mean, so has everything else. Everything's been weird. So I'm kind of used to it."

Again they drove in silence before Jeff said, "Can I ask you something?"

"All right." Henry glanced over at him.

"What about Bette?"

Hearing her name, which hadn't been mentioned once since Henry moved back home, made his foot lift off the gas. He smiled and shook his head. "Oh boy, you asked the question, all right. Well, how much do you know?"

"Your mom told me about Mathew."

"About them sleeping together?" Henry felt he needed to say it; he figured it would help him get over it.

"Yeah."

"Yeah, well, that was that."

"So you don't want anything to do with her anymore?" Jeff was looking at him.

Henry shrugged and sighed. "What choice do I have?"

Jeff turned and looked back out the window and they drove probably half a mile before he said, "People have gotten over worse stuff than that, you know. So don't rule her out so quick. I mean, if you don't want to."

Mathew stepped into Henry's room one afternoon to set down a stack of laundry and got sidetracked by the mess. At first he bent down and picked up the clothing that lay around the room; then he went over and started making his brother's disaster of a bed. The sheets were in a twisted clump near the foot and he straightened them out and pulled them up taut. Then he took hold of the pillow, which was folded up in a ball in the corner, and while he was shaking it back into shape a small square of shiny paper fell out of the pillowcase and drifted down to the floor. He stooped and picked it up and when he turned it over there she was. It was one of those little pictures taken in a photo booth. With lousy color and unnatural lighting.

She was smiling in the picture, looking right at the camera with those blue eyes.

He quickly tucked the photo back into the pillowcase and finished making Henry's bed. His heart was going like mad. Pumping and pounding as he stacked his brother's laundry on the bed. Then he hurried out of the room.

He didn't sleep well that night. And it wasn't really the thought of Bette's face that kept him awake (though the photo certainly brought her bright prettiness back to him). It was more about Henry. It was about his brother sleeping with that little photo of Bette Mack, pulling it out to look at it before going to sleep at night. Just the thought of it made Mathew's chest start aching again in the dark and made him start wishing all over again that he'd flown out of bed the night she slid in.

We'd been out twice before. Just out for some drives where I'd sit beside him in his truck among an odd assortment of tools and beer cans and crumpled-up cigarette packages and we'd drive out of town, along back roads, past farms and views and woods. My eye had started to ache to see things again. Land mostly. But cows too and swaybacked barns and people's Christmas lights hanging around their doors. I'd sit there and look out and feel wrenched with a kind of nostalgia. I guess nostalgia just for the world itself.

It was the middle of December when we took our third drive. A raw day with a blank white sky and his heater going the whole time, blowing dry musty air into our faces. We drove a few towns north, all on back roads, then on the way home he turned onto one of the main drags, lined with McDonald's and Burger Kings and car dealers. Jeff pointed out a new supermarket, one of those massive ones that have everything in them, and after we'd gone about a quarter of a mile past I said, "Let's go back. I want to look at it." It had been so long since I'd been in a store. And this one was a good forty-five minutes out of town, so I figured it was a safe bet I wasn't going to see anyone I knew. He turned the truck around and we went back.

Out of habit I got a cart and we walked slowly up and down the aisles. I was surprised at how much stuff I ended up throwing in there. Things I'd forgotten about, like English muffins and marmalade. A *Newsweek*. A bag of Pepperidge Farm cookies. It wasn't until I got to the last aisle that I realized I didn't have any money on me.

"I've got cash," Jeff told me, and took his wallet out of his back pocket. He cracked it open and was looking inside, when I glanced up and saw her appear around the corner down at the far end of the aisle. I froze. She was chewing gum and pushing a cart and scanning the milk section with her eyes narrowed. Then she looked up and saw me and came to an abrupt stop. I could tell she was thinking, her mind working fast before she turned and fled.

And it took me until that night to figure it out. The difference in her face and body. Her walk. It had all seemed odd until it finally occurred to me that she was pregnant.

Chapter 16

"It's sort of supposed to be an angel." Henry had his hands deep in his jacket pockets.

The reverend was frowning down at the little sculpture on his desk. "Ah, well, now that you say it, yes, I see. I see."

"I mean, since I don't know that much about them, I guess it's sort of my own version."

"Well, I thank you, Henry." The reverend looked up at Henry and smiled. "I'm very touched to have it. It's quite lovely."

Henry shrugged. He looked down at the little piece. It was made out of wire and feathers. While he was making it he thought about wings and kindness (the two things he'd always associated with angels), and what he wound up with was half Bette, half sparrow. A girl with long flowing hair and feathers sprouting from her arms. It surprised him how sad he felt giving it away. "I hope it's not like an insult or anything."

"An insult? Why would you think that?"

"Well, I know it doesn't exactly look like your run-of-the-mill angel."

"No. I wouldn't say it does, but belief calls for somewhat of a creative mind. Without that, let's face it, there'd be little reason to believe."

"Welp." Henry shrugged. "Anyway, Merry Christmas."

"Please, Henry." The reverend gestured to the chair across from his desk. "Have a seat, let's chat a bit. Do you have a minute?"

"Uh." Henry took his hands out of his pockets. "Sure." He sat down.

There was a little Christmas tree in the corner behind the reverend's desk and while Henry talked about what had been going on he kept looking over at it. It was lopsided with a handful of paper cutout decorations dangling from its scrawny limbs. Henry wondered if just looking at the thing was what made him wind up sounding as low as he did. Even though everything he was saying was fairly positive, about how he and his brother were better friends now than they'd ever been. How his mother had a new friend (he didn't mention any names), and this seemed to make her happier. But in the end it surprised him how flat and downtrodden he still sounded.

"And have you seen your father yet?" the reverend asked him at one point.

"Yet? You mean, have I gone to England?" Henry smiled.

The reverend looked concerned suddenly; he sat back in his chair and sighed. "I'm sorry. I thought you knew he was back."

"Back? You mean back here?"

Reverend Desell nodded sadly. "I saw him last week in the hardware store. I didn't speak with him but I did see him."

Henry sat still in the chair and looked over towards the Christmas tree. After a while he shook his head. "He wasn't like this," he said quietly. "I mean, my whole life he wasn't sneaky like this at all. It's so weird."

The room was quiet for a minute. Henry could hear a snowplow scraping the road out in front of the church.

He shook his head. "It's unbelievable. Why doesn't he call or anything? I just don't get it."

"I don't know." The reverend sighed and pressed his palms together. "Maybe he's scared. Maybe he's scared he's not wanted. I don't know."

"Well, he's right about that."

Reverend Desell leaned forward in his chair and touched the little angel gently with both his hands. He gave it a kind smile. "Oh, I'm not so convinced."

Something had come over his mother. A few mornings ago Mathew noticed when she walked into the kitchen that everything about her seemed to have sharpened and come back into focus. Suddenly the haze that had draped itself over her for months had vanished. Her voice, her walk, the way she sat down and ate her breakfast. It was all with a force behind it, no longer a kind of drifting.

Then as he was starting dinner one afternoon she suddenly came into the kitchen with her coat and gloves on. "I'm going out," she announced. "I'll be back in a while."

"Out?" Mathew couldn't help looking stunned. Since June she hadn't left the house on her own. "Out where?"

She was irritated and let him know. "I have something I have to take care of."

"But . . ." he heard himself say. She was already heading out the door. Her heels hammering down the walk. Her car starting with a roar and backing out of the driveway.

At first I wasn't going to do anything at all. I was thinking it wasn't my business and I should stay out of it. But business had nothing to do with it. The fact was my blood started howling like a locked-up, lonely dog. It took hold of me. Kidnapped me. I could feel that baby in my own belly. Feel her in my arms, smell her, hear her tiny butterfly breath.

When Bette's mother opened her front door that night, I was standing outside holding my hands together in front of me. "Mrs. Mack, I'm Augusta Iris," I said. "I was hoping to be able to speak with Bette."

She stood there for what felt like forever, a tall blond beautiful woman whose hard life had worked its way into her expression. She looked at me. I could tell she wanted to shut the door. Just close it quietly and leave me out there. But then she sighed and pulled it farther open and I stepped inside.

She left me in the living room with their Christmas tree blinking wildly in the corner and after a few minutes Bette walked into the room with her belly leading the way. She stopped when she saw me.

She was reading my face, then she seemed to fall towards me and a second later we were hugging, not saying a thing, just hanging on to each other, there in her living room.

Henry had been sitting on one of the headstones in the cemetery down the road, smoking one of his four daily cigarettes. He'd been making more angel sculptures all day for lack of anything better to do and finally walked outside for some air. He'd been smoking in the cemetery since he was thirteen, five years now, and it had a certain sacred quality to him. Peaceful, set apart from the world around it. He sat on the headstone of a man he had never known, Charles Goodrith, who died years before he was even born, and he looked across all the other graves. He was thinking how being dead must be pretty easy compared to all the energy living took. Boring maybe, but less painful too. Not that he wished he was dead. He was beyond that now. But he had the feeling it was something that was good to think about, a kind of perspective. All this running around just to wind up in a box.

As he was walking home he noticed his neighbor Mr. Schulman standing in his garage with his hands on his hips. When he saw Henry out on the road, he called to him, "Want to buy a car?"

Henry stopped and smiled. "As a matter of fact," he said, and started walking towards Mr. Schulman, "I do."

It wasn't what he had planned on buying at all. It was a yellow Cadillac Eldorado convertible that had started to rust on both front fenders. But suddenly, as he stood in the Schulmans' warm well-lit garage, the car struck Henry as a kind of answer. It was perfect. It was huge and ridiculous. He couldn't imagine driving the thing and feeling depressed. It was too humorous.

Mr. Schulman looked worried. "I wasn't actually serious, Henry," he said. "It *is* for sale but I'm not so sure you want to buy it."

Henry ran his hand over the door. "I think I might."

"Well, I think you better discuss it with your . . ." Mr. Schulman paused. "Anyway, you better think this over. You realize you can't drive it in bad weather, right? The top won't even go up anymore."

"Well, that's okay actually," Henry said. "I don't mind." He had his hood pulled up over his head and he stood and stared at the car for a second, then turned back to Mr. Schulman, who was neatly put-together in a bright green sweater and a pressed pair of khakis. "How much?" Henry asked.

"Well," Mr. Schulman said, "I was going to ask two but . . ."

"Fifteen and it's off your back," Henry said, his heart banging away in his chest.

"Gee, Henry, shouldn't you think about this? Don't you want to drive it?"

"Does it run?"

"Well, yes, it runs nicely but—"

"Fine. I'll take it. Do you mind cash?"

"Cash?" Mr. Schulman looked dumbstruck.

"Don't worry, it's not drug money or anything." Henry was smiling. "I just don't use a bank."

Mr. Schulman looked wary now. "I don't know about this. I hope your mother isn't angry with me for selling this to you."

"Oh, don't worry about my mom. It's my choice. She knows that."

Mr. Schulman shrugged. He didn't look happy at all.

"I'll be right back," Henry said. He took off at a run. He ran home, shuffled fifteen hundred dollars out of the large wad of lawn-mowing money in his desk drawer and ran back over to the Schulmans'.

"Can I take it, I mean with your plates, until I get new ones? I mean, I won't drive it far, just downtown and back."

Mr. Schulman sighed. "Are you sure about this, Henry?"

Henry was still breathing hard from running. He looked at the car. It was like a powerboat, long and wide and sleek. "Yup. I'm sure."

By the time Mr. Schulman had cleaned his stuff out of the car and had made a list for Henry of all the things that were wrong with it (he didn't ever want Henry to say he had not informed him properly), it was six o'clock and dark out.

Henry got into the car, started it up, and backed it slowly out of the Schulmans' garage. Mr. Schulman was standing where the car had been, both his hands in his pockets, looking plagued with uncertainty. Henry waved and pulled out onto the road. He wasn't accustomed to driving something so large and it took him a bit to get used to it. He drove past his house and onto the main road. He'd only been in a convertible a couple of times in his life and he'd forgotten how breezy it was. At one point he looked up and was surprised to see the trees pouring over his head and above them the sky and stars.

He drove through town, then turned around in the supermarket parking lot and drove back towards the house. He reached down and pushed the radio on and Aretha Franklin came booming clearly out through the two back speakers, and when he drove into the driveway the music rose up into the air around him. He leaned forward and put the car in park. A second later another car pulled in behind him, first just a flood of headlights in his rearview mirror; then it pulled up beside him and there Bette was, sitting in the passenger seat of his mother's Honda, smiling over at him. She rolled down the window and yelled over the music. "Nice car!"

His mother pulled her car forward and a second later Bette got out and came walking towards him through the big beams of his headlights. By the time she reached his door he'd gone into shock so all-body powerful that his mouth was dangling open, his eyes were widened and locked onto her belly.

"Catching flies," he heard her say, but suddenly the very concept of language was as out of reach to him as the stars in the sky over his head.

That night Mathew dreamed that Bette came into his room again. She was talking too loud and he kept telling her to talk quieter so no one would hear. "But why?" she asked him. She was sitting on the side of his bed and her leg was touching his. He couldn't think straight. "Because of your health," he heard himself say. This made her start to laugh.

By six o'clock the next morning he had two decent-sized duffels packed and he was on the side of his meticulously made bed looking down at the rug. He'd been sitting there for close to half an hour, waiting for it to get light out. Thinking about Bette. Everything about her was still a kind of disruption to his system. Not only her pregnancy, which caused his breath to leave him for what felt like minutes (the first thing she said to him was, "Don't worry, it's Henry's, I'm already six months"), but also her eyes and hair, her hands. Her voice. He just didn't know how he could do it. Live in the same house with her and feel normal. He was drawn to her. That was the biggest problem. And he felt it showed. He felt as if Henry could see it practically pouring from him. All that yearning.

So leaving seemed to be the only thing to do. But at the same time, he barely could get up off the bed and pick up the duffel bags and shut the lights out and walk into the hall. His limbs felt leaden with the very thought of it.

He moved slowly past his mother's bedroom, past Henry's door, down the stairs. He lowered each foot gently to each step, trying to avoid the whines in the wood. He had only a few vague ideas of where it was he might go. Back to school was the most obvious, maybe to find another apartment. Either that or to the Berkshires, where he'd been a couple of times as a kid. Maybe to stay at some motel somewhere for a few weeks. He could barely think about it, though. Just the thought of being in his car made his stomach feel as hollowed out as a gourd.

At the bottom of the stairs he turned and started through the dark living room, but he didn't get halfway before he heard something move on the couch. He stopped and stared. Sure enough, he could just make her out. Her belly rising up like a basketball in the middle of her body. She made a murmuring sound; then the room was quiet again. He was frozen. Half because he didn't want to wake her up but half because she was just lying there, and he loved her, loved her in his bones and blood.

"Are you thinking about killing me or something?" she whispered.

"Oh, sorry." He was startled she was awake. "I didn't want to wake you up."

He heard her yawn. "That's okay, I actually don't seem to sleep much anymore anyway. I mean it's kind of hard to sleep when someone's pummeling you in the gut. Do you usually get up this early now?" She yawned again.

"Uh," Mathew said, "well no, not usually."

She didn't say anything, she just sat up very slowly and reached over and turned on the light. It struck the room. He blinked down at her and she squinted up at him. She was wearing a pink flannel pajama suit with attached feet. It looked like a rabbit's suit. There were dark half-moons cradling her eyes. "Oh," she said. She was looking at his bags. "What are you doing?"

"Uhm, I guess I'm sort of, actually, leaving."

Her eyes opened wider. " 'Cause of me?" And then suddenly she was crying. Just like that. Tears everywhere, her whole body jerking from it. Mathew put his bags down and stood there. He didn't know what to do. She had her face cupped in her hands and she was leaning forward, bawling out and out.

"Bette," he said. "Jesus. Why are you crying?"

She shook her head and just kept on crying.

"Not because I'm leaving?"

He saw her nod.

"But . . ."

She took her hands away from her wet face and looked up at him. " 'Cause it's your home, Mathew! You can't just leave. I can't stand it. If you leave then I'll leave too. I can't stand that I hurt you like that. I didn't mean to hurt you." And then she collapsed again into another bout of sobs.

Mathew opened his mouth. His whole chest was tight. "Oh God," he was whispering in a hoarse voice, "you didn't hurt me. For crying out loud, Bette. It was the opposite of that." He stopped and looked down at the floor. "I'm leaving more because I thought everyone else would do better if I wasn't around. I thought maybe I'd get in the way."

She shook her head again. "You just can't go," she said. "If you go I'll go and I can't stand leaving again."

He walked over and sat down beside her. She smelled of oatmeal. He was about to put his arm around her to comfort her but she beat him to it; she leaned right into him, threw her arms around his waist, tucked her face in his chest, and kept on crying.

The first night Bette came back I dreamed there was a nun out on the lawn. I saw her from the living room window and I hurried out onto the porch because I knew right off she was waiting for me. When I got out there she was farther away suddenly, out towards the road, her two hands hanging at her sides like white napkins against her black habit. She said, "Yes?" just as I was about to say the same thing. "Yes, what is it?" Like I had been the one waiting for her. It made me stop for a minute, confused.

Then suddenly I realized there was something I wanted to ask her. I said, "Am I here?"

She had a mean face up until then but once I asked the question her eyes warmed and she smiled.

"Of course you are. You are right here." For a moment I felt at ease and then I heard something, a kind of humming sound coming from around the side of the house, and I walked down on the lawn and saw that Gordie was standing back there digging a hole, humming. He wasn't humming in a happy way. It was a frightening noise, almost a kind of buzzing.

"Gordie!" I said loudly.

But he just kept digging up the earth and piling it and digging deeper.

I woke up terrified. Mourning my own passing. I felt he was digging a grave, and I supposed it was for me.

I practically jumped off the mattress into the middle of the room. I was breathing hard. Oh God, I kept thinking. Oh God. Then suddenly there was a gentle knock on my door and it pushed open and Jeff was standing there with a ridiculous-looking ski hat on his head and his old army jacket. "Are you just getting up?" He was smiling. "It's almost ten."

I put my hand out and he gave me a baffled look as he walked up and took it. He took it in both his cold hands and asked, "What is it?"

"A nightmare," I said.

And then—I'm not quite sure how it happened—he paused and smiled, then leaned down and kissed me. And it wasn't until that moment, when his mouth was up against mine, that I realized I'd never kissed anybody but Gordie. And I imagine it was a little like finding a new door in a house you've lived in all your life and opening it and discovering a whole new light-filled room of your own.

Chapter 17

Henry practically forgot he'd even bought the car. That's how thrown off he was. The baby was the first thing he thought about when he opened his eyes in the mornings and practically the only thing he thought about until he closed them at night. He thought about it constantly and yet had almost nothing to go on. He'd never even held a baby as far as he could remember. So it was pure creativity on his part that allowed him to imagine what it would look like and act like and sound like. And every bit of it terrified him.

His initial feeling, the first night she came back, was to hightail it somewhere. Just blow out of town and never look back. He lay the entire night in his room feeling wildly frantic. Several times he literally sprang out of bed and started pacing back and forth. It was almost as if there was no place to put it. Just the thought of it. He couldn't think about it. And yet it was all he could think of.

And then he'd think of Bette, too. She was right there on the couch downstairs and when he'd remind himself of her he would come close to feeling relieved. But then he'd think of her belly and the baby inside and it would blossom larger than anything else among his thoughts.

The first two days were like that. Like having the wind knocked out of him and being unable to get his breath back. He couldn't get comfortable. He didn't even feel hungry. He'd turn on Bob Dylan but then the minute he heard his whiny voice he'd turn him off. He'd go out for a walk but by the time he reached the end of the driveway he'd turn around and walk back again. He was a wreck.

Finally, on the third night, after everyone had gone to sleep, he got out of bed and crept down the stairs. He stood in the doorway of the living room in the dark and looked at her lying on the couch. He could just make her out. After a minute he whispered, "Bette?"

She sat right up and said, "Yup," like she'd been waiting for him.

He stood for another second, then walked over and sat down on the couch near her feet. He looked out into the dark. His heart was going. He could feel her looking at him.

"Henry," she finally whispered, "you have to tell me if you want me here. I mean, forget the baby part and tell me if you're at all happy to see me."

"That's the thing," he said in a hoarse whisper. He still wasn't looking at her. "The thing is I've wanted you back here ever since you left. I mean, underneath my being pissed off and everything, underneath it, I've missed you. You know, like a lot. And I want you back. I'm just so freaked out."

"About the baby?"

He nodded. He couldn't have said the word if he'd tried.

"I get you," she said.

"I mean, I don't even know where to put it in my head. It's like I'm totally ill equipped for this. Totally." He looked over at her. His eyes had now adjusted to the dark and he could see her right there looking at him.

"I understand," she said softly.

"I mean, if you had a choice at this point, I'd be pleading for you to get an abortion. There wouldn't be any question in my mind."

She nodded. "I know. I actually did go to have one. I knew that's what you would have wanted. I actually drove to the place, Henry, and sat in the parking lot, but I realized I was going against everything I felt. Not stuff in my head or stuff I believed in. But I just wanted this kid. That's all it came down to in the end. *I* wanted it."

He sat for a minute looking down in his lap. Then he shook his head slowly and smiled. "Jesus Christ," he said, "I feel like I can't even breathe I'm so scared."

They sat there for a long time without saying anything; then he stood up and walked towards the door. "Henry," she said, "if you don't feel different in a week or two, I'll go back home. It won't end the world or anything if you decide you're not ready."

He didn't say a thing. He just walked quietly out of the room and up the stairs. When he got into his room he shut the door gently and went over and sat on the side of his bed. He took a deep breath. Then he put his face into his hands.

It was around nine-thirty in the morning and Mathew was cleaning up some of the breakfast dishes. Henry hadn't come down yet and his mother had come and gone and Bette was still sitting at the table in his mother's blue bathrobe, looking at the newspaper. He was planning on making a big salad for lunch and was putting it together in his mind and at the same time thinking how the upstairs bathroom needed to be cleaned. Then someone knocked at the side door.

He shut off the water in the sink and dried his hands on his apron and opened the door, and there, standing on the step in a green down jacket that didn't look familiar, was his father. Mathew just stood there looking at him through the storm door. He was too surprised to do anything else. Finally his father said, "Mathew? Can I come in?"

"Oh," Mathew said, and stepped back to open the door.

"Holy mackerel," he heard Bette say behind him as his father took a few halting steps inside.

The first thing Mathew thought was that he'd shrunk. Not only did he look shorter but smaller too. His face and head. He stood near the doorway and kept his hands in his pockets.

"Dad?" Mathew managed to say. "What's going on?"

His father shrugged and shook his head.

"Dad?" Mathew said quietly.

"Is your mother here, Mathew?" His voice was murky, as if it were coming from some dark part of him.

"I'll go and get her," Bette said, hurrying off. Only then did Mathew realize she'd been standing there in her bathrobe, obviously not knowing what to do.

"Who's that?" his father said, obviously trying to distract himself.

"That's Henry's girlfriend."

His father nodded. "How's school?"

"Well, I uh, I haven't been there for a while actually, I kind of took the fall off."

His father nodded again, as if he were processing information but it wasn't touching him in any way.

"Why don't you come inside, Dad." Mathew stepped towards the kitchen. "Have a cup of coffee or something."

His father glanced up and smiled sadly and shook his head. "Thanks, Matty," he said. "I think I'll just stay here."

A second later his mother came into the kitchen, her face tangled with worry and fear and sadness. Bette was behind her, looking almost as anxious. "Gordie?" His mother's voice was quiet.

"Oh Augusta," his father said, almost pleadingly.

Mathew and Bette glanced at each other and then both headed out towards the living room. When they got there they froze, listening hard for the two voices, but they couldn't hear a thing. "Wow," Bette whispered. "I've got goose bumps now."

Mathew shook his head. He felt weak and he walked over and sat down in a chair near the fireplace. Bette sat quietly on the couch. "What do you think he's saying?" she whispered.

He shook his head again. "I really don't know."

They sat there in silence for a few minutes; then they heard Henry's door open upstairs. Mathew stood up quickly and went to the stairs. Henry was halfway down them. "Henry," he said, "Dad's here."

Henry, who had looked half asleep up until then, seemed to snap to attention. "He's here?"

"Yeah, he's talking to Mom. He doesn't look so good."

Henry stood still for a minute, making up his mind about something; then he said, "Well," and sat down on the stairs.

Mathew went up the stairs, sidestepping Henry. When he got into his room he shut the door softly and sat down on his bed. He sat very still for a while, listening for some kind of sound. But the house was quiet. Then he leaned over and opened his night table drawer and pulled his father's old rabbit's foot out. He held it for a minute, locked it inside his palm, went back downstairs, sidestepping Henry's slouched body again. He went out the back door and crossed the lawn. His father's car was still sitting in the driveway and Mathew glanced towards the kitchen door to make sure he wasn't about to come outside; then he opened the car door and hung the raunchy little thing from his rearview mirror, so that it dangled there and couldn't be missed.

We didn't sit down or walk into the kitchen. We just stood there near the door. He looked like a ghost of himself. Gaunt and pale. There in front of me but pretty much missing altogether. "What's happened to you?" was the first thing out of my mouth. I felt stunned, shaken up to see him looking that bad.

He shook his head. "Marion left me," he said and I saw his face go slack with pain.

It seemed that he was cut loose from his life. As lost as I'd ever seen anyone. I suppose if he'd asked to come back I would have let him. I probably wouldn't have thought too hard about it either. I would have led him back up to the room and had him lie down. He looked so tired.

But it was obvious after a few minutes, after he told me how she'd up and deserted him, that whatever he'd hoped for by coming back here wasn't going to happen. I saw the disappointment start in his forehead and slowly work its way like a fire down his face.

It was a terrible thing. Watching him walk back out to the car a little while later. His shoulders folded in, his feet in the shoes I'd given him for Christmas a year back making their way across the driveway to his car. I stood there on the step in the cold with my arms folded over my chest and I watched while he started the car and backed out onto the road. It was only a couple of days before Christmas. He hadn't even asked how Henry was.

On the way back to my room I found Henry sitting alone on the stairs. He didn't look up. He sat slumped over his knees, not moving. I looked at him from the bottom of the steps for a minute; then I went up and sat down beside him. He sat so still I couldn't even hear his breathing. I was remembering how he used to sit on the stairs when he was younger and go through his baseball cards. He'd organize them step by step until the whole staircase was covered with them. He'd spend entire afternoons whistling under his breath, going up and down and back up, his hair falling into his eyes, his nose always needing to be blown.

After a long while of just sitting there next to him I reached out and took hold of his hand and I pulled it onto my lap and held it in both of mine. I had let go of him months ago, around the same time I suppose I'd let go of Gordie. For no good reason at all I'd abandoned him, too.

Finally I said, "Henry, tell me you're all right."

A second later I noticed a tear fall onto the step between his feet, then a second later a bigger one hit next to the first. Then a second after that he nodded and said, "Yup, I'm okay," and his hand came to life and took hold of mine.

For some reason it was the one thought that hadn't entered his head. It simply didn't occur to him until that night, the night of the day his father came to the house. He was up in his bedroom at his desk, the door shut, smoking a cigarette (since Bette had come back he'd broken his four-a-day pact and was back up to half a pack), when it dawned on him that he was going to be this kid's father. Of course he'd known he was the father but he hadn't thought about being a father. Actually being one and being looked at by this kid as one. And suddenly there it was, something he could actually envision, and not just the thought of being a father. But being a loving father, a great father, a father like he'd never known and never until that moment imagined. It was nothing more than a tiny bead of light. Just a mere pinpoint really, far in the distance. But after what felt like miles of nothing but grim darkness his eyes locked onto it and without a moment's hesitation he felt himself start heading its way.

Bette was sitting in the kitchen eating a bowl of cereal and reading *People* magazine when Mathew opened the letter from Harvard.

She wasn't even facing him, so she couldn't see his expression as he read, but when he refolded the letter and slipped it back into its envelope, without turning around, still crunching on her cereal, she said, "Yes, well, so what's it say?"

He was used to this by now. Nothing slipped past her. He was convinced she had some sort of internal radar that kept track of everyone around her. He slipped the letter into his apron. "Not much," he told her.

She looked at him with her eyebrows raised. "Yeah, right, and my father's the Pope. What's it say? That you got to go back or else, right?"

He sighed, then reluctantly slipped the letter out of his apron and handed it over.

"Thank you," she said pertly, and read it while continuing to eat her cereal. After she was done she folded it back up and passed it over her shoulder to him. She didn't say anything for a couple of minutes. She went back to her magazine and he went back to the dishes. Then she said, "Well. You only live once, might as well do whatever makes you less miserable."

He smiled into the dirty pot he was scrubbing. He'd figured that was what she was going to say.

But he was off balance for the rest of the afternoon. Lopsided from the letter he kept in the front pocket of his apron, no heavier than an eggshell but burdening him like a bowling ball.

The day before Christmas I packed all his things in boxes, I suppose the way widows do. Cleaned his drawers and took all his old suits and his shoes out of the closet. I packed the pair of glasses he'd been wearing the day I first met him. Packed the fly-fishing kit he'd never used. His camera. His sweaters. I even dumped out the odds and ends that were in the drawer of his night table—a handful of paper clips, a bottle of aspirin, a train schedule.

At first I was going to put all the boxes in the basement, but once I got down there I realized that not only was it damp but it was too crowded already and I didn't want us having to sidestep all of Gordie's things every time we went down. So I decided to bring everything to the studio where I didn't have to see it. I got my boots and jacket on and went out the back door and trudged through the snow with a box in my arms. When I reached the studio I pulled the big wooden door open and stepped into the room and when I looked up I was so struck by what I saw that the box dropped clear out of my hands and went crashing and rattling across the floor. It frightened me at first. The vision of the room in front of me. Not only the huge sculpture in the middle of it that rose clear to the ceiling but the dozen other smaller ones that sat around the studio, on windowsills and on the floor and on the workbench. It took me a minute to get my bearings. I stood there with Gordie's belongings at my feet and my mouth open like a pitcher and I blinked around me. What I saw was an entire room filled with wings that were held out to the air as if they were about to start beating. Massive wings and minuscule ones, wings thick as doors and others thin as dragonflies. It was a room as still as a corpse and yet it was verging on an absolute explosion of flight.

Except for Jeff, who came in with a big basket of fruit and nuts for everyone, no one bought presents, so it wasn't much of a Christmas. But Henry could still sense the holiday in the air. When he stuck his head out the door that morning there wasn't a drop of sound coming from the road or the sky, the way it gets only on Christmas.

Bette went back to her mother's house for the morning. His mother drove her down and was going to pick her up around two o'clock. But by noon Henry had started to feel her absence. The house was too quiet, and when he walked past the couch in the living room with her bags neatly arranged beside it and the comforter she'd been sleeping under folded at the end, he just stopped and stood there. He leaned down and carefully unzipped one of her bags and out came the delicate smell of her. Half powdery and half just Bette. He scratched his head.

Except for the one conversation he'd had with her he'd still managed to keep his distance. Every time he saw her it was like being thrown into a headlock and he just couldn't seem to act calm and natural. Plagued at moments by thoughts of her with Mathew and at other moments torpedoed with thoughts of the baby. His baby right there inside her. It made him go all heartbeat and silent just at the sight of her.

His mother and Jeff were sitting at the kitchen table when he walked in that afternoon and Mathew was rolling dough out on the counter, his glasses cockeyed on his face.

"Mom," Henry said.

She looked up from the newspaper she'd been reading.

"What time are you supposed to pick up Bette?"

"Two." She looked up at the clock. "In twenty minutes."

"I thought maybe you guys might want to take a ride in my car."

Jeff looked up and grinned.

"I mean, it's nice out and we could pick her up on the way."

"I'd love it," Mathew said. "I need some air."

"Well, you'll get air all right." Jeff laughed. "We'd better bundle up, this isn't exactly convertible weather."

"Yup, hats are a necessity," Henry said.

Ten minutes later they were all piled in the car, Augusta and Jeff in the back seat and Mathew next to Henry in the front. They all had hats and heavy jackets on. As Henry pulled out onto the main road he heard Jeff holler behind him, "Hey, let's drive to Florida!"

Henry drove slowly down through town. At one point he glanced over at Mathew, who was hunched up with a large scarf wrapped around his neck and a big red wool ski cap pulled down to his eyebrows. "What do you think?" Henry yelled over at him.

"I think it's just wonderful!" Mathew said. "It's great!"

His mother had to give him directions to Bette's house since he'd never once been there. And when he heard her say from the back seat, "Right here, that green one there on the left," his heart sank. It was a lousy house, its lime-green paint peeling, two garbage cans turned over on the lawn, a rusted-out Dodge Dart parked next to Bette's white Nova, which evidently wasn't running anymore. When Henry pulled into the driveway nobody said a thing, they all just quietly looked towards the door.

A minute later Bette came sailing out of the house and started to laugh when she saw them all sitting in the car in the driveway. "God, I wish I had a camera!" she said. "You guys look hysterical."

Henry suddenly looked up and saw her mother through the big bay window. He'd never even spoken to her. She was standing with her hands on her hips, looking at them all. She didn't look amused. Bette waved to her before she got in the car but her mother just turned and walked away from the window.

Mathew got out to let Bette slide in next to Henry. It was the closest they'd been to each other. "This is great!" she shouted. "Can't we drive around a bit before we go back home?"

"That's the plan," Henry said.

They drove out of town, past the school, along the ridge where Henry and Bette had watched the fireworks that first night. Probably the night she got pregnant, Henry thought. First night they were together. He remembered unbuttoning her shirt, each pearly button slipping silently through its buttonhole, and the way he parted her blouse and sort of dove towards her, like he was plunging out of a burning building into a big beautiful swimming pool.

He kept his eyes on the road but his whole body was conscious of her next to him and of his kid inside her, curled like a tadpole. He went around one corner and he felt her slip away from him towards Mathew, so on the next corner, this one the other direction, he took it a little harder so that she slid back against him. Then he took a silent breath, his heart beating, the wind swirling around them, and he lifted his right hand off the steering wheel and dropped it gently onto her leg.

Mathew had been wavering for days about what to do. And finally that morning he woke up with a decision. He was going back to school. There was no reason not to. No good reason anyway. So he made his mind up, laid it in his head like a brick wall, and got out of bed.

Then that afternoon, while riding in Henry's convertible, they came to a curve in the road that caused Bette Mack's body to slide slightly across the seat towards him. When the road straightened out she shifted back a bit towards Henry but a second later Mathew noticed her leg had remained up against his. Just touching slightly. And it stayed that way for the rest of the ride, with him half thinking he was imagining it and half knowing he wasn't. Even after he saw his brother's hand drop onto her left leg, and her hand reach out and cover it, her right leg remained against his, gentle but unyielding, maybe quietly letting him know he was part of things too, needed, no longer alone, and hopefully not going anywhere.

When we were almost back home, I felt Henry take his foot off the gas and we started to coast down Pinter Hill Road, first slowly, then gathering momentum, and in the end flying, hurtling, all our hats being tugged by the wind. Three quarters of the way down Bette suddenly stood up and screamed at the top of her lungs. Just sprang up and let out a scream that was so high-pitched and wild it almost sounded like a whistle; then she plunked back down in her seat and turned around and looked at me. She yelled, "Sorry! But I just had to get that out of my system."

It was a scream that flew into the air behind us like a wild set-free bird, containing everything, joy and misery and simply release, simply the feeling that we were together, an odd kind of herd, plummeting through the cold Christmas afternoon air. A scream, I was figuring, like the one that baby was going to let out with her first gulp of the world, wild and crazed from not knowing what was up ahead. But at the same time, somehow, knowing the worst was behind her.